EVERYMAN, I will go with thee,

and be thy guide,

In thy most need to go by thy side

NIKOLAY VASILYEVICH GOGOL

Born at Sorochintsy, Russia, on 19th March
(Old Style) 1809, Government official,
teacher, lecturer at St Petersburg University.
Writer and thinker. Lived in Rome from
1837 to 1848. Died on 21st February (O.S.)
1852 in Moscow.

NIKOLAY GOGOL

Taras Bulba

TRANSLATED BY
C. J. HOGARTH

INTRODUCTION BY
JOHN COURNOS

DENT: LONDON
EVERYMAN'S LIBRARY
DUTTON: NEW YORK

All rights reserved
Printed in Great Britain
at the
Aldine Press · Letchworth · Herts
for
J. M. DENT & SONS LTD
Aldine House · Bedford Street · London
'Taras Bulba' first published in
Everyman's Library 1918
Last reprinted 1962

NO. 1740

INTRODUCTION

RUSSIAN literature contains no greater creative mystery than Nikolay Vasilyevich Gogol (1809–52), who did for the Russian novel and Russian prose what Pushkin did for Russian poetry. Before these two men came Russian literature can hardly have been said to exist. It was pompous and effete with pseudo-classicism; foreign influences were strong; in the speech of the upper circles there was an over-fondness for German, French and English words. Between them the two friends cleared away the debris which made for sterility and erected in their stead a new structure out of living Russian words. Coming up from Little Russia, the Ukraine, with Cossack blood in his veins, Gogol injected his own healthy virus into an effete body, blew his own virile spirit, the spirit of his race, into its nostrils and gave the Russian novel its direction to this very day.

More than that. The nomad and romantic in him, troubled and restless with Ukrainian myth, legend and song, impressed upon Russian literature, faced with the realities of modern life, a spirit titanic and in clash with its material, and produced in the mastery of this everyday material, commonly called sordid, a phantasmagoria intense with beauty. A clue to all Russian realism may be found in a Russian critic's observation about Gogol: 'Seldom has nature created a man so romantic in bent, yet so masterly in portraying all that is unromantic in life.' But this statement does not cover the whole ground, for it is easy to see in almost all of Gogol's work his 'free Cossack soul' trying to break through the shell of sordid today like some ancient demon, essentially Dionysian. So that his works, true though they are to our life, are at once a reproach, a protest and a challenge, ever calling for joy, ancient joy, that is no more with us. And they have all the joy and sadness of the Ukrainian songs he loved so much.

Indeed, so great was his enthusiasm for his own land that after collecting material for many years, the year 1833 finds him at work on a history of 'poor Ukraine', a work planned to take up six volumes. Furthermore, he intended to follow this work with a universal history in eight volumes with a view to establishing, as far as may be gathered, Little Russia and the world in proper relation.

Too much a visionary and a poet to be an impartial historian, it is hardly astonishing to note the judgment he passes on his own work in 1834: 'My history of Little Russia is an extraordinarily mad thing, and it could not be otherwise.' The deeper he goes into Little Russia's past the more fanatically he dreams of Little Russia's future. St Petersburg wearies him, Moscow awakens no emotion in him, he yearns for Kieff, the mother of Russian cities, which in his vision he sees becoming 'the Russian Athens'. Russian history gives him no pleasure, and he separates it definitely from Ukrainian history. During his seven-year stay in St Petersburg (1829–36) Gogol zealously gathered historical material. How completely he dis-associated Ukraine from Northern Russia may be judged by the

conspectus of his lectures written in 1832. He says in it, speaking of
the conquest of Southern Russia in the fourteenth century by Prince
Guedimin at the head of his Lithuanian host, still dressed in the
skins of wild beasts, still worshipping the ancient fire and practising
pagan rites: 'Then Southern Russia, under the mighty protection of
Lithuanian princes, completely separated itself from the North.
Every bond between them was broken; two kingdoms were estab-
lished under a single name—Russia—one under the Tatar yoke, the
other under the same rule with Lithuanians. But actually they had
no relation with one another; different laws, different customs,
different aims, different bonds and different activities gave them
wholly different characters.'

This same Prince Guedimin freed Kieff from the Tatar yoke. This
city had been laid waste by the hordes of Ghengis Khan and hidden
for a very long time from the Slavonic chronicler as behind an
impenetrable curtain. A shrewd man, Guedimin appointed a Slavonic
prince to rule over the city and permitted the inhabitants to practise
their own faith, Greek Christianity. Prior to the Mongol invasion,
which brought conflagration and ruin, and subjected Russia to a
two-century bondage, cutting her off from Europe, a state of chaos
existed and the separate tribes fought with one another constantly
and for the most petty reasons. Mutual depredations were possible
owing to the absence of mountain ranges; there were no natural
barriers against sudden attack. The openness of the steppe made the
people warlike. But this very openness made it possible later for
Guedimin's pagan hosts, fresh from the fir forests of what is now
White Russia, to make a clean sweep of the whole country between
Lithuania and Poland, and thus give the scattered princedoms a
much-needed cohesion. In this way Ukraine was formed. Whether
you looked to the north towards Russia, to the east towards the
Tatars, to the south towards the Crimean Tatars, to the west
towards Poland, everywhere the country bordered on a field, everywhere on a plain, which left it open to the invader from every side.
Had there been here, suggests Gogol in his introduction to his never-
written history of Little Russia, if upon one side only, a real frontier
of mountain or sea, the people who settled here might have formed a
definite political body. Without this natural protection it became a
land subject to constant attack and despolation.

This constant menace acted at last like a fierce hammer shaping
and hardening resistance against itself. The fugitive from Poland, the
fugitive from the Tatar and the Turk, homeless, with nothing to lose,
their lives ever exposed to danger, forsook their peaceful occupations
and became transformed into a warlike people, known as the Cossacks, whose appearance towards the end of the thirteenth century
or at the beginning of the fourteenth was a remarkable event which
possibly alone prevented any further inroads by the two Mohamme-
dan nations into Europe. The appearance of the Cossacks was
coincident with the appearance in Europe of brotherhoods and
knighthood-orders, and this new race, in spite of its living the life of

marauders, in spite of turning its foes' tactics on its foes, was not free of the religious spirit of its time; if it warred for its existence it warred not less for its faith, which was Greek. Indeed, as the nation grew stronger and became conscious of its strength, the struggle began to partake something of the nature of a religious war, not alone defensive but aggressive also, against the unbeliever. While any man was free to join the brotherhood it was obligatory to believe in the Greek faith. It was this religious unity, blazed into activity by the presence across the borders of unbelieving nations, that alone indicated the germ of a political body in this gathering of men, who otherwise lived the audacious lives of a band of highway robbers.

Little by little the community grew and with its growing it began to assume a general character. The beginning of the sixteenth century found whole villages settled with families, enjoying the protection of the Cossacks, who exacted certain obligations, chiefly military, so that these settlements bore a military character. The sword and the plough were friends which fraternized at every settler's. On the other hand, the gay bachelors began to make depredations across the border to sweep down on Tatars' wives and their daughters and to marry them.

All of Ukraine took on its colour from the Cossack, and if I have drawn largely on Gogol's own account of the origins of this race, it was because it seemed to me that Gogol's emphasis on the heroic rather than on the historical would give the reader a proper approach to the mood in which he created *Taras Bulba*, the finest epic in Russian literature. Gogol never wrote either his history of Little Russia or his universal history. Apart from several brief studies, not always reliable, the net result of his many years' application to his scholarly projects was this brief epic in prose, Homeric in mood. Into this short work he poured all his love of the heroic, all his romanticism, all his poetry, all his joy.

Yet *Taras Bulba* was in a sense an accident, just as many other works of great men are accidents. It often requires a happy combination of circumstances to produce a masterpiece. Just as *Dead Souls* might never have been written if *Don Quixote* had not existed, so there is every reason to believe that *Taras Bulba* could not have been written without the *Odyssey*. Once more ancient fire gave life to new beauty. And yet at the time Gogol could not have had more than a smattering of the *Odyssey*. The magnificent translation made by his friend Zhukovsky had not yet appeared and Gogol, in spite of his ambition to become an historian, was not equipped as a scholar. But it is evident from his dithyrambic letter on the appearance of Zhukovsky's version, forming one of the famous series of letters known as *Correspondence with Friends*, that he was better acquainted with the spirit of Homer than any mere scholar could be. Is not the *Odyssey*, he asks, in every sense a deep reproach to our nineteenth century?

An understanding of Gogol's point of view gives the key to *Taras Bulba*. For in this panoramic canvas of the *Setch*, the military brotherhood of the Cossacks, living under open skies, picturesquely and heroically, he has drawn a picture of his romantic ideal, which if far from perfect at any rate seemed to him preferable to the grey tedium of a city peopled with government officials.

JOHN COURNOS.

SELECT BIBLIOGRAPHY

SEPARATE WORKS (titles in English; dates of first publication in Russian). *Evenings on a Farm near Dikanka* (including 'Sorochinsky Fair', 'St John's Eve', 'A May Night', 'The Lost Letter', 'Christmas Eve', 'The Terrible Vengeance', 'Ivan Sponka and his Aunt', 'A Place Bewitched'), 1831; *Mirgorod* (including 'The Old-world Landowner', 'Taras Bulba', 'The Story of the Quarrel between Ivan Ivanovich and Ivan Nikiforovich'), 1835; *Diary of a Madman*, 1835; *The Carriage*, 1836; *The Nose*, 1836; *The Inspector General*, 1836; *Dead Souls*, 1842; *Nevsky Prospect*, 1842; *The Portrait*, 1842; *The Overcoat*, 1842; *Marriage*, 1842; *Gamblers*, 1842; *The Lawsuit*, 1842; *Meditations on the Divine Liturgy* (posthumously published), 1855; 'His Inner Conflict' (selections from letters in *A Treasury of Russian Life and Humour*, edited by J. Cournos, New York), 1943.

COLLECTED WORKS. Translated by Constance Garnett, 6 vols., 1922–9.

BIOGRAPHY AND CRITICISM. J. Lavrin, *Gogol*, 1926; C. Manning, 'Nicholas Gogol' in *The Slavonic Review*, iv, 12, 1926; M. Joslin, *N. V. Gogol and E. T. A. Hoffmann*, 1933; R. L. Brazol, *The Mighty Three*, 1934; A. Kaun, 'Poe and Gogol: a Comparison', in *The Slavonic Review*, xv, 44, 1937; V. V. Nabokov, *Nikolai Gogol*, 1944; S. Bertensen, 'The Première of *The Inspector General*', in *The Russian Review*, vii, 1, 1947; C. Lefevre, 'Gogol and Anglo-Russian Literary Relations during the Crimean War', in *The American Slavic Review*, viii, 2, 1949; J. Lavrin, *Nikolai Gogol (1809–1852): A Centenary Survey*, 1951; C. Cizevsky, 'The Unknown Gogol', in *The Slavonic Review*, xxx, 75, 1952; 'Gogol, Artist and Thinker', in *The Annals of the Ukrainian Academy of Arts and Sciences in the United States*, ii, 2, 1952; N. Brodiansky, 'Gogol and his Characters', in *The Slavonic Review*, xxxi, 76, 1952; H. E. Bowman, 'The Nose', in *The Slavonic Review*, xxxi, 76, 1952; T. Shebunina, 'Gogol Yesterday and Today', in *The Anglo-Soviet Journal*, xiii, 2, 1952; M. Rylsky, 'A Versatile Genius', in *The Anglo-Soviet Journal*, xiii, 2, 1952; V. V. Yermilov, 'One of the Greatest Names in our Literature', in *The Anglo-Soviet Journal*, xiii, 2, 1952; S. Petrov, 'A Great Humanist', in *The Anglo-Soviet Journal*, xiii, 2, 1952; L. I. Strahovsky, 'The Historianism of Gogol', in *The American Slavic Review*, xii, 3, 1953; C. Bryner, 'Gogol's *The Overcoat* in World Literature', in *The Slavonic Review*, xxxii, 79, 1954; R. L. Strong, 'The Soviet Interpretation of Gogol', in *The American Slavic Review*, xiv, 4, 1955; M. H. Futrell, 'Gogol and Dickens', in *The Slavonic Review*, xxxiv, 83, 1956; D. Magarshack, *Gogol, a Life*, 1957.

Other studies of Gogol will be found in the following general histories of Russian literature and thought: K. Waliszewski, *A History of Russian Literature*, 1897; A Bruckner, *A Literary History of Russia*, 1908; M. Baring, *Landmarks in Russian Literature*, 1910; Le Vicomte E.-M. de Vogüé, *The Russian Novel*, 1913; P. Kropotkin, *Russian Literature, Ideals and Realities*, 1916; M. Baring, *An Outline of Russian Literature*, 1929; I. Spectar, *The Golden Age of Russian Literature*, 1943; R. Hare, *Russian Literature from Pushkin to the Present Day*, 1947; D. Mirsky, *A History of Russian Literature*, 1949; M. Slonim, *The Epic of Russian Literature*, 1950; V. Zenkovsky, *A History of Russian Philosophy*, 1953.

TARAS BULBA

I

"Turn round, my boy! How ridiculous you look! What sort of a priest's cassock have you got on? Does everybody at the academy dress like that?"

With such words did old Bulba greet his two sons, who had been absent for their education at the Royal Seminary of Kief, and had now returned home to their father.

His sons had but just dismounted from their horses. They were a couple of stout lads who still looked bashful, as became youths recently released from the seminary. Their firm healthy faces were covered with the first down of manhood, down which had, as yet, never known a razor. They were greatly discomfited by such a reception from their father, and stood motionless with eyes fixed upon the ground.

"Stand still, stand still! let me have a good look at you," he continued, turning them round. "How long your gaberdines are! What gaberdines! There never were such gaberdines in the world before. Just run, one of you! I want to see whether you will not get entangled in the skirts, and fall down."

"Don't laugh, don't laugh, father!" said the eldest lad at length.

"How touchy we are! Why shouldn't I laugh?"

"Because, although you are my father, if you laugh, by heavens, I will strike you!"

"What kind of a son are you? what, strike your father!" exclaimed Taras Bulba, retreating several paces in amazement.

"Yes, even my father. I don't stop to consider persons when an insult is in question."

"So you want to fight me? with your fist, eh?"

"Any way."

"Well, let it be fisticuffs," said Taras Bulba, turning up his sleeves. "I'll see what sort of a man you are with your fists."

And father and son, in lieu of a pleasant greeting after long separation, began to deal each other heavy blows on ribs, back, and chest, now retreating and looking at each other, now attacking afresh.

"Look, good people! the old man has gone mad! he has lost his senses completely!" screamed their pale, ugly, kindly mother, who was standing on the threshold, and had not yet succeeded in embracing her darling children. "The children have come home, we have not seen them for over a year; and now he has taken some strange freak—he's pommelling them."

"Yes, he fights well," said Bulba, pausing; "well, by heavens!" he continued, rather as if excusing himself, "although he has never tried his hand at it before, he will make a good Cossack! Now, welcome, son! embrace me," and father and son began to kiss each other. "Good lad! see that you hit every one as you pommelled me; don't let any one escape. Nevertheless your clothes are ridiculous all the same. What rope is this hanging here?—And you, you lout, why are you standing there with your hands hanging beside you?" he added, turning to the youngest. "Why don't you fight me? you son of a dog!"

"What an idea!" said the mother, who had managed in the meantime to embrace her youngest. "Who ever heard of children fighting their own father? That's enough for the present; the child is young, he has had a long journey, he is tired." The child was over twenty, and about six feet high. "He ought to rest, and eat something; and you set him to fighting!"

"You are a gabbler!" said Bulba. "Don't listen to your mother, my lad; she is a woman, and knows

nothing. What sort of petting do you need? A clear
field and a good horse, that's the kind of petting for
you! And do you see this sword? that's your mother!
All the rest people stuff your heads with is rubbish;
the academy, books, primers, philosophy, and all that,
I spit upon it all!" Here Bulba added a word which is
not used in print. "But I'll tell you what is best: I'll
take you to Zaporozhe [1] this very week. That's where
there's science for you! There's your school; there
alone will you gain sense."

"And are they only to remain at home a week?"
said the worn old mother sadly and with tears in her
eyes. "The poor boys will have no chance of looking
around, no chance of getting acquainted with the home
where they were born; there will be no chance for me
to get a look at them."

"Enough, you've howled quite enough, old woman!
A Cossack is not born to run around after women.
You would like to hide them both under your petticoat,
and sit upon them as a hen sits on eggs. Go, go, and let
us have everything there is on the table in a trice.
We don't want any dumplings, honey-cakes, poppy-
cakes, or any other such messes: give us a whole sheep,
a goat, mead forty years old, and as much corn-brandy
as possible, not with raisins and all sorts of stuff, but
plain scorching corn-brandy, which foams and hisses
like mad."

Bulba led his sons into the principal room of the hut;
and two pretty servant girls wearing coin necklaces,
who were arranging the apartment, ran out quickly.
They were either frightened at the arrival of the young
men, who did not care to be familiar with any one; or
else they merely wanted to keep up their feminine
custom of screaming and rushing away headlong at
the sight of a man, and then screening their blushes for
some time with their sleeves. The hut was furnished
according to the fashion of that period—a fashion

[1] The Cossack country beyond (za) the falls (porozhe) of the
Dnieper.

concerning which hints linger only in the songs and lyrics, no longer sung, alas! in the Ukraine as of yore by blind old men, to the soft tinkling of the native guitar, to the people thronging round them—according to the taste of that warlike and troublous time, of leagues and battles prevailing in the Ukraine after the union. Everything was cleanly smeared with coloured clay. On the walls hung sabres, hunting-whips, nets for birds, fishing-nets, guns, elaborately carved powder-horns, gilded bits for horses, and tether-ropes with silver plates. The small window had round dull panes, through which it was impossible to see except by opening the one movable one. Around the windows and doors red bands were painted. On shelves in one corner stood jugs, bottles, and flasks of green and blue glass, carved silver cups, and gilded drinking vessels of various makes—Venetian, Turkish, Tscherkessian, which had reached Bulba's cabin by various roads, at third and fourth hand, a thing common enough in those bold days. There were birch-wood benches all around the room, a huge table under the holy pictures in one corner, and a huge stove covered with parti-coloured patterns in relief, with spaces between it and the wall. All this was quite familiar to the two young men, who were wont to come home every year during the dog-days, since they had no horses, and it was not customary to allow students to ride afield on horseback. The only distinctive things permitted them were long locks of hair on the temples, which every Cossack who bore weapons was entitled to pull. It was only at the end of their course of study that Bulba had sent them a couple of young stallions from his stud.

Bulba, on the occasion of his sons' arrival, ordered all the sotniks or captains of hundreds, and all the officers of the band who were of any consequence, to be summoned; and when two of them arrived with his old comrade, the Osaul or sub-chief, Dmitro Tovkatch, he immediately presented the lads, saying, "See what fine young fellows they are! I shall send them to the

Setch [1] shortly." The guests congratulated Bulba and the young men, telling them they would do well and that there was no better knowledge for a young man than a knowledge of that same Zaporozhian Setch.

" Come, brothers, seat yourselves, each where he likes best, at the table; come, my sons. First of all, let's take some corn-brandy," said Bulba. " God bless you! Welcome, lads; you, Ostap, and you, Andríi. God grant that you may always be successful in war, that you may beat the Mussulmans and the Turks and the Tatars; and that when the Poles undertake any expedition against our faith, you may beat the Poles. Come, clink your glasses. How now? Is the brandy good? What's corn-brandy in Latin? The Latins were stupid: they did not know there was such a thing in the world as corn-brandy. What was the name of the man who wrote Latin verses? I don't know much about reading and writing, so I don't quite know. Wasn't it Horace? "

" What a dad! " thought the elder son Ostap. " The old dog knows everything, but he always pretends the contrary."

" I don't believe the archimandrite allowed you so much as a smell of corn-brandy," continued Taras. " Confess, my boys, they thrashed you well with fresh birch-twigs on your backs and all over your Cossack bodies; and perhaps, when you grew too sharp, they beat you with whips. And not on Saturday only, I fancy, but on Wednesday and Thursday."

" What is past, father, need not be recalled; it is done with."

" Let them try it now," said Andríi. " Let anybody just touch me, let any Tatar risk it now, and he'll soon learn what a Cossack's sword is like! "

" Good, my son, by heavens, good! And when it comes to that, I'll go with you; by heavens, I'll go too! What should I wait here for? To become a buckwheat-

[1] The village or, rather, permanent camp of the Zaporozhian Cossacks.

reaper and housekeeper, to look after the sheep and swine, and loaf around with my wife? Away with such nonsense! I am a Cossack; I'll have none of it! What's left but war? I'll go with you to Zaporozhe to carouse; I'll go, by heavens!" And old Bulba, growing warm by degrees and finally quite angry, rose from the table, and, assuming a dignified attitude, stamped his foot. "We will go to-morrow! Wherefore delay? What enemy can we besiege here? What is this hut to us? What do we want with all these things? What are pots and pans to us?" So saying, he began to knock over the pots and flasks, and to throw them about.

The poor old woman, well used to such freaks on the part of her husband, looked sadly on from her seat on the wall-bench. She did not dare say a word; but when she heard the decision which was so terrible for her, she could not refrain from tears. As she looked at her children, from whom so speedy a separation was threatened, it is impossible to describe the full force of her speechless grief, which seemed to quiver in her eyes and on her lips convulsively pressed together.

Bulba was terribly headstrong. He was one of those characters which could only exist in that fierce fifteenth century, and in that half-nomadic corner of Europe, when the whole of Southern Russia, deserted by its princes, was laid waste and burned to the quick by pitiless troops of Mongolian robbers; when men deprived of house and home grew brave there; when, amid conflagrations, threatening neighbours, and eternal terrors, they settled down, and growing accustomed to looking these things straight in the face, trained themselves not to know that there was such a thing as fear in the world; when the old, peaceable Slav spirit was fired with warlike flame, and the Cossack state was instituted—a free, wild outbreak of Russian nature—and when all the river-banks, fords, and like suitable places were peopled by Cossacks, whose number no man knew. Their bold comrades had a right to reply to the Sultan when he asked how many they were,

" Who knows? We are scattered all over the steppes: wherever there is a hillock, there is a Cossack.''

It was, in fact, a most remarkable exhibition of Russian strength, forced by dire necessity from the bosom of the people. In place of the original provinces with their petty towns, in place of the warring and bartering petty princes ruling in their cities, there arose great colonies, kuréns,[1] and districts, bound together by one common danger and hatred against the heathen robbers. The story is well known how their incessant warfare and restless existence saved Europe from the merciless hordes which threatened to overwhelm her. The Polish kings, who now found themselves sovereigns, in place of the provincial princes, over these extensive tracts of territory, fully understood, despite the weakness and remoteness of their own rule, the value of the Cossacks, and the advantages of the warlike, untrammelled life led by them. They encouraged them and flattered this disposition of mind. Under their distant rule, the hetmans or chiefs, chosen from among the Cossacks themselves, redistributed the territory into military districts. It was not a standing army, no one saw it; but in case of war and general uprising, it required a week, and no more, for every man to appear on horseback, fully armed, receiving only one ducat from the king; and in two weeks such a force had assembled as no recruiting officers would ever have been able to collect. When the expedition was ended, the army dispersed among the fields and meadows and the fords of the Dnieper; each man fished, wrought at his trade, brewed his beer, and was once more a free Cossack. Their foreign contemporaries rightly marvelled at their wonderful qualities. There was no handicraft which the Cossack was not expert at: he could distil brandy, build a waggon, make powder, and do blacksmith's and gunsmith's work, in addition to committing wild excesses, drinking and carousing as only a Russian can—all this he was equal to. Besides

[1] Cossack villages. In the Setch, a large wooden barrack.

the registered Cossacks, who considered themselves bound to appear in arms in time of war, it was possible to collect at any time, in case of dire need, a whole army of volunteers. All that was required was for the Osaul or sub-chief to traverse the market-places and squares of the villages and hamlets, and shout at the top of his voice, as he stood in his waggon, " Hey, you distillers and beer-brewers! you have brewed enough beer, and lolled on your stoves, and stuffed your fat carcasses with flour, long enough! Rise, win glory and warlike honours! You ploughmen, you reapers of buckwheat, you tenders of sheep, you danglers after women, enough of following the plough, and soiling your yellow shoes in the earth, and courting women, and wasting your warlike strength! The hour has come to win glory for the Cossacks! " These words were like sparks falling on dry wood. The husbandman broke his plough; the brewers and distillers threw away their casks and destroyed their barrels; the mechanics and merchants sent their trade and their shop to the devil, broke the pots and everything else in their homes, and mounted their horses. In short, the Russian character here received a profound development, and manifested a powerful outward expression.

Taras was one of the band of old-fashioned leaders; he was born for warlike emotions, and was distinguished for his uprightness of character. At that epoch the influence of Poland had already begun to make itself felt upon the Russian nobility. Many had adopted Polish customs, and began to display luxury in splendid staffs of servants, hawks, huntsmen, dinners, and palaces. This was not to Taras's taste. He liked the simple life of the Cossacks, and quarrelled with those of his comrades who were inclined to the Warsaw party, calling them serfs of the Polish nobles. Ever on the alert, he regarded himself as the legal protector of the orthodox faith. He entered despotically into any village where there was a general complaint of oppression by the revenue farmers and of the addition of fresh

taxes on necessaries. He and his Cossacks executed
justice, and made it a rule that in three cases it was
absolutely necessary to resort to the sword. Namely,
when the commissioners did not respect the superior
officers and stood before them covered; when any one
made light of the faith and did not observe the customs
of his ancestors; and, finally, when the enemy were
Mussulmans or Turks, against whom he considered it
permissible, in every case, to draw the sword for the
glory of Christianity.

Now he rejoiced beforehand at the thought of how
he would present himself with his two sons at the Setch,
and say, " See what fine young fellows I have brought
you!" how he would introduce them to all his old
comrades, steeled in warfare; how he would observe
their first exploits in the sciences of war and of drinking,
which was also regarded as one of the principal warlike
qualities. At first he had intended to send them forth
alone; but at the sight of their freshness, stature, and
manly personal beauty his martial spirit flamed up
and he resolved to go with them himself the very next
day, although there was no necessity for this except his
obstinate self-will. He began at once to hurry about and
give orders; selected horses and trappings for his sons,
looked through the stables and storehouses, and chose
servants to accompany them on the morrow. He
delegated his power to Osaul Tovkatch, and gave with
it a strict command to appear with his whole force at
the Setch the very instant he should receive a message
from him. Although he was jolly, and the effects of his
drinking bout still lingered in his brain, he forgot nothing.
He even gave orders that the horses should be watered,
their cribs filled, and that they should be fed with the
finest corn; and then he retired, fatigued with all his
labours.

" Now, children, we must sleep, but to-morrow we
shall do what God wills. Don't prepare us a bed: we
need no bed; we will sleep in the courtyard."

Night had but just stole over the heavens, but Bulba

always went to bed early. He lay down on a rug and covered himself with a sheepskin pelisse, for the night air was quite sharp and he liked to lie warm when he was at home. He was soon snoring, and the whole household speedily followed his example. All snored and groaned as they lay in different corners. The watchman went to sleep the first of all, he had drunk so much in honour of his young masters' home-coming.

The mother alone did not sleep. She bent over the pillow of her beloved sons, as they lay side by side ; she smoothed with a comb their carelessly tangled locks, and moistened them with her tears. She gazed at them with her whole soul, with every sense ; she was wholly merged in the gaze, and yet she could not gaze enough. She had fed them at her own breast, she had tended them and brought them up; and now to see them only for an instant! " My sons, my darling sons! what will become of you? what fate awaits you? " she said, and tears stood in the wrinkles which disfigured her once beautiful face. In truth, she was to be pitied, as was every woman of that period. She had lived only for a moment of love, only during the first ardour of passion, only during the first flush of youth; and then her grim betrayer had deserted her for the sword, for his comrades and his carouses. She saw her husband two or three days in a year, and then, for several years, heard nothing of him. And when she did see him, when they did live together, what a life was hers! She endured insult, even blows; she felt caresses bestowed only in pity; she was a misplaced object in that community of unmarried warriors, upon which wandering Zaporozhe cast a colouring of its own. Her pleasureless youth flitted by; her ripe cheeks and bosom withered away unkissed and became covered with premature wrinkles. Love, feeling, everything that is tender and passionate in a woman, was converted in her into maternal love. She hovered around her children with anxiety, passion, tears, like the gull of the steppes. They were taking her sons, her darling sons, from her——taking them from her, so that she should never see them again! Who knew? Perhaps a Tatar would cut off their heads in the very first skirmish, and she would never know where their deserted bodies might lie, torn by birds of prey ; and yet for each single drop of their blood she would have given all hers. Sobbing, she gazed into their eyes, even when all-powerful sleep began to close them, and thought, " Perhaps Bulba, when he wakes, will put off their departure for a day or two; perhaps it occurred to him to go so soon because he had been drinking."

The moon from the summit of the heavens had long since lit up the whole courtyard filled with sleepers, the thick clump of willows, and the tall steppe-grass, which hid the palisade surrounding the court. She still sat at her sons' pillow, never removing her eyes from them for a moment, nor thinking of sleep. Already the horses, divining the approach of dawn, had ceased eating and lain down upon the grass; the topmost leaves of the willows began to rustle softly, and little by little the rippling rustle descended to their bases. She sat there until daylight, unwearied, and wishing in her heart that the night might prolong itself indefinitely. From the steppes came the ringing neigh of the horses, and red streaks shone brightly in the sky. Bulba suddenly awoke, and sprang to his feet. He remembered quite well what he had ordered the night before. " Now, my men, you've slept enough! 'tis time, 'tis time! Water the horses! And where is the old woman? " He generally called his wife so. " Be quick, old woman, get us something to eat; the way is long."

The poor old woman, deprived of her last hope, slipped sadly into the hut.

Whilst she, with tears, prepared what was needed for breakfast, Bulba gave his orders, went to the stable, and selected his best trappings for his children with his own hand.

The scholars were suddenly transformed. Red morocco boots with silver heels took the place of their dirty old ones; trousers wide as the Black Sea, with

countless folds and plaits, were kept up by golden
girdles from which hung long slender thongs, with
tassels and other tinkling things, for pipes. Their
jackets of scarlet cloth were girt by flowered sashes
into which were thrust engraved Turkish pistols; their
swords clanked at their heels. Their faces, already a
little sunburnt, seemed to have grown handsomer and
whiter; their slight black moustaches now cast a more
distinct shadow on this pallor and set off their healthy,
youthful complexions. They looked very handsome in
their black sheepskin caps, with cloth-of-gold crowns.

When their poor mother saw them, she could not utter
a word, and tears stood in her eyes.

" Now, my lads, all is ready; no delay! " said Bulba
at last. " But we must first all sit down together, in
accordance with Christian custom before a journey."

All sat down, not excepting the servants, who had
been standing respectfully at the door.

" Now, mother, bless your children," said Bulba.
" Pray God that they may fight bravely, always defend
their warlike honour, always defend the faith of Christ;
and, if not, that they may die, so that their breath may
not be longer in the world."

" Come to your mother, children; a mother's prayer
protects on land and sea."

The mother, weak as mothers are, embraced them,
drew out two small holy pictures, and hung them,
sobbing, around their necks. " May God's mother—
keep you! Children, do not forget your mother—send
some little word of yourselves——" She could say no
more.

" Now, children, let us go," said Bulba.

At the door stood the horses, ready saddled. Bulba
sprang upon his " Devil," which bounded wildly, on
feeling on his back a load of over thirty stone, for Taras
was extremely stout and heavy.

When the mother saw that her sons were also
mounted, she rushed towards the younger, whose
features expressed somewhat more gentleness than

those of his brother. She grasped his stirrup, clung to his saddle, and with despair in her eyes, refused to loose her hold. Two stout Cossacks seized her carefully, and bore her back into the hut. But before the cavalcade had passed out of the courtyard, she rushed with the speed of a wild goat, quite disproportionate to her years, to the gate, stopped a horse with irresistible strength, and embraced one of her sons with mad, unconscious violence. Then they led her away again.

The young Cossacks rode on sadly, repressing their tears out of fear of their father, who, on his side, was somewhat moved, although he strove not to show it. The morning was grey, the green sward bright, the birds twittered rather discordantly. They glanced back as they rode. Their paternal farm seemed to have sunk into the earth. All that was visible above the surface were the two chimneys of their modest hut and the tops of the trees up whose trunks they had been used to climb like squirrels. Before them still stretched the field by which they could recall the whole story of their lives, from the years when they rolled in its dewy grass down to the years when they awaited in it the dark-browed Cossack maiden, running timidly across it on quick young feet. There is the pole above the well, with the waggon wheel fastened to its top, rising solitary against the sky; already the level which they have traversed appears a hill in the distance, and now all has disappeared. Farewell, childhood, games, all, all, farewell!

II

ALL three horsemen rode in silence. Old Taras's thoughts were far away: before him passed his youth, his years —the swift-flying years, over which the Cossack always weeps, wishing that his life might be all youth. He wondered whom of his former comrades he should meet at the Setch. He reckoned up how many had already

died, how many were still alive. Tears formed slowly
in his eyes, and his grey head bent sadly.

His sons were occupied with other thoughts. But we
must speak further of his sons. They had been sent,
when twelve years old, to the academy at Kief, because
all leaders of that day considered it indispensable to
give their children an education, although it was afterwards utterly forgotten. Like all who entered the
academy, they were wild, having been brought up
in unrestrained freedom; and whilst there they had
acquired some polish, and pursued some common
branches of knowledge which gave them a certain
resemblance to each other.

The elder, Ostap, began his scholastic career by
running away in the course of the first year. They
brought him back, whipped him well, and set him down
to his books. Four times did he bury his primer in the
earth; and four times, after giving him a sound thrashing, did they buy him a new one. But he would no
doubt have repeated this feat for the fifth time, had not
his father given him a solemn assurance that he would
keep him at monastic work for twenty years, and sworn
in advance that he should never behold Zaporozhe all
his life long, unless he learned all the sciences taught in
the academy. It was odd that the man who said this
was that very Taras Bulba who condemned all learning, and counselled his children, as we have seen, not
to trouble themselves at all about it. From that
moment, Ostap began to pore over his tiresome books
with exemplary diligence, and quickly stood on a level
with the best. The style of education in that age
differed widely from the manner of life. The scholastic,
grammatical, rhetorical, and logical subtilties in vogue
were decidedly out of consonance with the times, never
having any connection with, and never being encountered in, actual life. Those who studied them, even the
least scholastic, could not apply their knowledge to
anything whatever. The learned men of those days were
even more incapable than the rest, because farther

removed from all experience. Moreover, the republican constitution of the academy, the fearful multitude of young, healthy, strong fellows, inspired the students with an activity quite outside the limits of their learning. Poor fare, or frequent punishments of fasting, with the numerous requirements arising in fresh, strong, healthy youth, combined to arouse in them that spirit of enterprise which was afterwards further developed among the Zaporozhians. The hungry student running about the streets of Kief forced every one to be on his guard. Dealers sitting in the bazaar covered their pies, their cakes, and their pumpkin-rolls with their hands, like eagles protecting their young, if they but caught sight of a passing student. The consul or monitor, who was bound by his duty to look after the comrades entrusted to his care, had such frightfully wide pockets to his trousers that he could stow away the whole contents of the gaping dealer's stall in them. These students constituted an entirely separate world, for they were not admitted to the higher circles, composed of Polish and Russian nobles. Even the Waiwode, Adam Kisel, in spite of the patronage he bestowed upon the academy, did not seek to introduce them into society, and ordered them to be kept more strictly in supervision. This command was quite superfluous, for neither the rector nor the monkish professors spared rod or whip; and the lictors sometimes, by their orders, lashed their consuls so severely that the latter rubbed their trousers for weeks afterwards. This was to many of them a trifle, only a little more stinging than good vodka with pepper: others at length grew tired of such constant blisters, and ran away to Zaporozhe if they could find the road and were not caught on the way. Ostap Bulba, although he began to study logic, and even theology, with much zeal, did not escape the merciless rod. Naturally, all this tended to harden his character, and give him that firmness which distinguishes the Cossacks. He always held himself aloof from his comrades.

He rarely led others into such hazardous enterprises

as robbing a strange garden or orchard; but, on the
other hand, he was always among the first to join the
standard of an adventurous student. And never, under
any circumstances, did he betray his comrades; neither
imprisonment nor beatings could make him do so. He
was unassailable by any temptations save those of war
and revelry; at least, he scarcely ever dreamt of any
others. He was upright with his equals. He was kind-
hearted, after the only fashion that kind-heartedness
could exist in such a character and at such a time. He
was touched to his very heart by his poor mother's
tears; but this only vexed him, and caused him to hang
his head in thought.

His younger brother, Andríi, had livelier and more
fully developed feelings. He learned more willingly,
and without the effort with which strong and weighty
characters generally have to make in order to apply
themselves to study. He was more inventive-minded
than his brother, and frequently appeared as the leader
of dangerous expeditions; sometimes, thanks to the
quickness of his mind, contriving to escape punishment
when his brother Ostap, abandoning all efforts, stripped
off his gaberdine and lay down upon the floor without
a thought of begging for mercy. He too thirsted for
action; but, at the same time, his soul was accessible to
other sentiments. The need of love burned ardently
within him. When he had passed his eighteenth year,
woman began to present herself more frequently in
his dreams; listening to philosophical discussions, he
still beheld her, fresh, black-eyed, tender; before him
constantly flitted her elastic bosom, her soft, bare arms;
the very gown which clung about her youthful yet well-
rounded limbs breathed into his visions a certain inexpressible sensuousness. He carefully concealed this
impulse of his passionate young soul from his comrades,
because in that age it was held shameful and dishonourable for a Cossack to think of love and a wife before he
had tasted battle. On the whole, during the last year,
he had acted more rarely as leader to the bands of

students, but had roamed about more frequently alone, in remote corners of Kief, among low-roofed houses, buried in cherry orchards, peeping alluringly at the street. Sometimes he betook himself to the more aristocratic streets, in the old Kief of to-day, where dwelt Little Russian and Polish nobles, and where the houses were built in more fanciful style. Once, as he was gaping along, an old-fashioned carriage belonging to some Polish noble almost drove over him; and the heavily moustached coachman, who sat on the box, gave him a smart cut with his whip. The young student fired up; with thoughtless daring he seized the hind-wheel with his powerful hands and stopped the carriage. But the coachman, fearing a drubbing, lashed his horses; they sprang forward, and Andríi, succeeding happily in freeing his hands, was flung full length on the ground with his face flat in the mud. The most ringing and harmonious of laughs resounded above him. He raised his eyes and saw, standing at a window, a beauty such as he had never beheld in all his life, black-eyed, and with skin white as snow illumined by the dawning flush of the sun. She was laughing heartily, and her laugh enhanced her dazzling loveliness. Taken aback he gazed at her in confusion, abstractedly wiping the mud from his face, by which means it became still further smeared. Who could this beauty be? He sought to find out from the servants, who, in rich liveries, stood at the gate in a crowd surrounding a young guitar-player; but they only laughed when they saw his besmeared face and deigned him no reply. At length he learned that she was the daughter of the Waiwode of Koven, who had come thither for a time. The following night, with the daring characteristic of the student, he crept through the palings into the garden and climbed a tree which spread its branches upon the very roof of the house. From the tree he gained the roof, and made his way down the chimney straight into the bedroom of the beauty, who at that moment was seated before a lamp, engaged in removing the costly earrings from her ears.

The beautiful Pole was so alarmed on suddenly beholding an unknown man that she could not utter a single word; but when she perceived that the student stood before her with downcast eyes, not daring to move a hand through timidity, when she recognised in him the one who had fallen in the street, laughter again overpowered her.

Moreover, there was nothing terrible about Andríi's features; he was very handsome. She laughed heartily, and amused herself over him for a long time. The lady was giddy, like all Poles; but her eyes—her wondrous clear, piercing eyes—shot one glance, a long glance. The student could not move hand or foot, but stood bound as in a sack, when the Waiwode's daughter approached him boldly, placed upon his head her glittering diadem, hung her earrings on his lips, and flung over him a transparent muslin chemisette with gold-embroidered garlands. She adorned him, and played a thousand foolish pranks, with the childish carelessness which distinguishes the giddy Poles, and which threw the poor student into still greater confusion.

He cut a ridiculous figure, gazing immovably, and with open mouth, into her dazzling eyes. A knock at the door startled her. She ordered him to hide himself under the bed, and, as soon as the disturber was gone, called her maid, a Tatar prisoner, and gave her orders to conduct him to the garden with caution, and thence show him through the fence. But our student this time did not pass the fence so successfully. The watchman awoke, and caught him firmly by the foot; and the servants, assembling, beat him in the street, until his swift legs rescued him. After that it became very dangerous to pass the house, for the Waiwode's domestics were numerous. He met her once again at church. She saw him, and smiled pleasantly, as at an old acquaintance. He saw her once more, by chance; but shortly afterwards the Waiwode departed, and, instead of the beautiful black-eyed Pole, some fat face or other gazed from the window. This was what Andríi was

thinking about, as he hung his head and kept his eyes
on his horse's mane.

In the meantime the steppe had long since received
them all into its green embrace; and the high grass,
closing round, concealed them, till only their black
Cossack caps appeared above it.

" Eh, eh, why are you so quiet, lads? " said Bulba at
length, waking from his own reverie. " You're like
monks. Now, all thinking to the Evil One, once for all!
Take your pipes in your teeth, and let us smoke, and
spur on our horses so swiftly that no bird can overtake
us."

And the Cossacks, bending low on their horses'
necks, disappeared in the grass. Their black caps were
no longer to be seen; a streak of trodden grass alone
showed the trace of their swift flight.

The sun had long since looked forth from the clear
heavens and inundated the steppe with his quickening,
warming light. All that was dim and drowsy in the
Cossacks' minds flew away in a twinkling: their hearts
fluttered like birds.

The farther they penetrated the steppe, the more
beautiful it became. Then all the South, all that region
which now constitutes New Russia, even as far as the
Black Sea, was a green, virgin wilderness. No plough
had ever passed over the immeasurable waves of wild
growth; horses alone, hidden in it as in a forest, trod
it down. Nothing in nature could be finer. The whole
surface resembled a golden-green ocean, upon which
were sprinkled millions of different flowers. Through
the tall, slender stems of the grass peeped light-blue,
dark-blue, and lilac star-thistles; the yellow broom
thrust up its pyramidal head; the parasol-shaped white
flower of the false flax shimmered on high. A wheat-ear,
brought God knows whence, was filling out to ripening.
Amongst the roots of this luxuriant vegetation ran
partridges with outstretched necks. The air was filled
with the notes of a thousand different birds. On high
hovered the hawks, their wings outspread, and their

eyes fixed intently on the grass. The cries of a flock of wild ducks, ascending from one side, were echoed from God knows what distant lake. From the grass arose, with measured sweep, a gull, and skimmed wantonly through blue waves of air. And now she has vanished on high, and appears only as a black dot: now she has turned her wings, and shines in the sunlight. Oh, steppes, how beautiful you are!

Our travellers halted only a few minutes for dinner. Their escort of ten Cossacks sprang from their horses and undid the wooden casks of brandy, and the gourds which were used instead of drinking vessels. They ate only cakes of bread and dripping; they drank but one cup apiece to strengthen them, for Taras Bulba never permitted intoxication upon the road, and then continued their journey until evening.

In the evening the whole steppe changed its aspect. All its varied expanse was bathed in the last bright glow of the sun; and as it grew dark gradually, it could be seen how the shadow flitted across it and it became dark green. The mist rose more densely; each flower, each blade of grass, emitted a fragrance as of ambergris, and the whole steppe distilled perfume. Broad bands of rosy gold were streaked across the dark blue heaven, as with a gigantic brush; here and there gleamed, in white tufts, light and transparent clouds: and the freshest, most enchanting of gentle breezes barely stirred the tops of the grass-blades, like sea-waves, and caressed the cheek. The music which had resounded through the day had died away, and given place to another. The striped marmots crept out of their holes, stood erect on their hind legs, and filled the steppe with their whistle. The whirr of the grasshoppers had become more distinctly audible. Sometimes the cry of the swan was heard from some distant lake, ringing through the air like a silver trumpet. The travellers, halting in the midst of the plain, selected a spot for their night encampment, made a fire, and hung over it the kettle in which they cooked their oatmeal; the steam rising and floating aslant in the air. Having supped, the Cossacks lay down to sleep, after hobbling their horses and turning them out to graze. They lay down in their gaberdines. The stars of night gazed directly down upon them. They could hear the countless myriads of insects which filled the grass; their rasping, whistling, and chirping, softened by the fresh air, resounded clearly through the night, and lulled the drowsy ear. If one of them rose and stood for a time, the steppe presented itself to him strewn with the sparks of glow-worms. At times the night sky was illumined in spots by the glare of burning reeds along pools or river-bank; and dark flights of swans flying to the north were suddenly lit up by the silvery, rose-coloured gleam, till it seemed as though red kerchiefs were floating in the dark heavens.

The travellers proceeded onward without any adventure. They came across no villages. It was ever the same boundless, waving, beautiful steppe. Only at intervals the summits of distant forests shone blue, on one hand, stretching along the banks of the Dnieper. Once only did Taras point out to his sons a small black speck far away amongst the grass, saying, " Look, children! yonder gallops a Tatar." The little head with its long moustaches fixed its narrow eyes upon them from afar, its nostrils, snuffing the air like a greyhound's, and then disappeared like an antelope on its owner perceiving that the Cossacks were thirteen strong. " And now, children, don't try to overtake the Tatar! You would never catch him to all eternity; he has a horse swifter than my Devil." But Bulba took precautions, fearing hidden ambushes. They galloped along the course of a small stream, called the Tatarka, which falls into the Dnieper; rode into the water and swam with their horses some distance in order to conceal their trail. Then, scrambling out on the bank, they continued their road.

Three days later they were not far from the goal of their journey. The air suddenly grew colder: they could feel the vicinity of the Dnieper. And there it gleamed afar, distinguishable on the horizon as a dark band. It sent forth cold waves, spreading nearer, nearer, and finally seeming to embrace half the entire surface of the earth. This was that section of its course where the river, hitherto confined by the rapids, finally makes its own way and, roaring like the sea, rushes on at will; where the islands, flung into its midst, have pressed it farther from their shores, and its waves have spread widely over the earth, encountering neither cliffs nor hills. The Cossacks, alighting from their horses, entered the ferry-boat, and after a three hours' sail reached the shores of the island of Khortitz, where at that time stood the Setch, which so often changed its situation.

A throng of people hastened to the shore with boats. The Cossacks arranged the horses' trappings. Taras assumed a stately air, pulled his belt tighter, and proudly stroked his moustache. His sons also inspected themselves from head to foot, with some apprehension and an undefined feeling of satisfaction; and all set out together for the suburb, which was half a verst from the Setch. On their arrival, they were deafened by the clang of fifty blacksmiths' hammers beating upon twenty-five anvils sunk in the earth. Stout tanners seated beneath awnings were scraping ox-hides with their strong hands; shop-keepers sat in their booths, with piles of flints, steels, and powder before them; Armenians spread out their rich handkerchiefs; Tatars turned their kabobs upon spits; a Jew, with his head thrust forward, was filtering some corn-brandy from a cask. But the first man they encountered was a Zaporozhetz [1] who was sleeping in the very middle of the road with legs and arms outstretched. Taras Bulba could not refrain from halting to admire him. "How splendidly developed he is; phew, what a magnificent figure!" he said, stopping his horse. It was, in fact, a striking picture. The Zaporozhetz had stretched himself out in

[1] Sometimes written Zaporovian.

the road like a lion; his scalp-lock, thrown proudly behind him, extended over upwards of a foot of ground; his trousers of rich red cloth were spotted with tar, to show his utter disdain for them. Having admired to his heart's content, Bulba passed on through the narrow street, crowded with mechanics exercising their trades, and with people of all nationalities who thronged this suburb of the Setch, resembling a fair, and fed and clothed the Setch itself, which knew only how to revel and burn powder.

At length they left the suburb behind them, and perceived some scattered kuréns,[1] covered with turf, or in Tatar fashion with felt. Some were furnished with cannon. Nowhere were any fences visible, or any of those low-roofed houses with verandahs supported upon low wooden pillars, such as were seen in the suburb. A low wall and a ditch, totally unguarded, betokened a terrible degree of recklessness. Some sturdy Zapo-rozhtzi lying, pipe in mouth, in the very road, glanced indifferently at them, but never moved from their places. Taras threaded his way carefully among them, with his sons, saying, " Good-day, gentles."—" Good-day to you," answered the Zaporozhtzi. Scattered over the plain were picturesque groups. From their weather-beaten faces, it was plain that all were steeled in battle, and had faced every sort of bad weather. And there it was, the Setch! There was the lair from whence all those men, proud and strong as lions, issued forth! There was the spot whence poured forth liberty and Cossacks over all the Ukraine.

The travellers entered the great square where the council generally met. On a huge overturned cask sat a Zaporozhetz without his shirt; he was holding it in his hands, and slowly sewing up the holes in it. Again their way was stopped by a whole crowd of musicians, in the midst of whom a young Zaporozhetz was dancing, with head thrown back and arms outstretched. He kept shouting, " Play faster, musicians! Begrudge not,

[1] Enormous wooden sheds, each inhabited by a troop or kurén.

Thoma, brandy to these orthodox Christians!" And
Thoma, with his blackened eye, went on measuring out
without stint, to every one who presented himself, a
huge jugful.

About the youthful Zaporozhetz four old men, moving
their feet quite briskly, leaped like a whirlwind to one
side, almost upon the musicians' heads, and, suddenly
retreating, squatted down and drummed the hard earth
vigorously with their silver heels. The earth hummed
dully all about, and afar the air resounded with national
dance tunes beaten by the clanging heels of their boots.
But one shouted more loudly than all the rest, and
flew after the others in the dance. His scalp-lock
streamed in the wind, his muscular chest was bare, his
warm, winter fur jacket was hanging by the sleeves,
and the perspiration poured from him as from a pail.
"Take off your jacket!" said Taras at length: "see
how he steams!"—"I can't," shouted the Cossack.
"Why?"—"I can't: I have such a disposition that
whatever I take off, I drink up." And indeed, the young
fellow had not had a cap for a long time, nor a belt to
his caftan, nor an embroidered neckerchief: all had
gone the proper road. The throng increased; more
folk joined the dancer: and it was impossible to observe
without emotion how all yielded to the impulse of that
dance, the freest, the wildest, the world has ever seen,
still called from its mighty originators, the Kosachka.

"Oh, if I had no horse to hold," exclaimed Taras,
"I would join the dance myself!"

Meanwhile there began to appear among the throng
men who were respected for their prowess throughout
all the Setch—old greyheads who had been leaders
more than once. Taras soon found a number of familiar
faces. Ostap and Andríi heard nothing but greetings.
"Ah, it is you, Petcheritza! Good day, Kozolup!"—
"Whence has God brought you, Taras?"—"How did
you come here, Doloto? Health to you, Kirdyaga!
Hail to you, Gustui! Did I ever think of seeing you,
Remen?" And these heroes, gathered from all the

roving population of Eastern Russia, kissed each other
and began to ask questions. " But what has become of
Kasyan? Where is Borodavka? and Koloper? and
Pidsuitok? " And in reply, Taras Bulba learned that
Borodavka had been hung at Tolopan, that Koloper
had been flayed alive at Kizikirmen, that Pidsuitok's
head had been salted and sent in a cask to Constantinople. Old Bulba hung his head and said thoughtfully,
" They were good Cossacks."

III

TARAS BULBA and his sons had been in the Setch about
a week. Ostap and Andríi occupied themselves but
little with the science of war. The Setch was not fond
of wasting time in warlike exercises. The young genera-
tion learned these by experience alone, in the very heat
of battles, which were therefore incessant. The Cossacks
thought it a nuisance to fill up the intervals of this
instruction with any kind of drill, except perhaps
shooting at a mark, and on rare occasions with horse-
racing and wild-beast hunts on the steppes and in the
forests. All the rest of the time was devoted to revelry
—a sign of the wide diffusion of moral liberty. The whole
of the Setch presented an unusual scene: it was one
unbroken revel; a ball noisily begun, which had no
end. Some busied themselves with handicrafts; others
kept little shops and traded; but the majority caroused
from morning till night, if the wherewithal jingled in
their pockets, and if the booty they had captured had
not already passed into the hands of the shopkeepers
and spirit-sellers. This universal revelry had something
fascinating about it. It was not an assemblage of topers,
who drank to drown sorrow, but simply a wild revelry
of joy. Every one who came thither forgot everything,
abandoned everything which had hitherto interested
him. He, so to speak, spat upon his past and gave

himself recklessly up to freedom and the good-fellow-
ship of men of the same stamp as himself—idlers having
neither relatives nor home nor family, nothing, in short,
save the free sky and the eternal revel of their souls.
This gave rise to that wild gaiety which could not have
sprung from any other source. The tales and talk current among the assembled crowd, reposing lazily on the
ground, were often so droll, and breathed such power
of vivid narration, that it required all the nonchalance
of a Zaporozhetz to retain his immovable expression,
without even a twitch of the moustache—a feature
which to this day distinguishes the Southern Russian
from his northern brethren. It was drunken, noisy
mirth; but there was no dark ale-house where a man
drowns thought in stupefying intoxication: it was a
dense throng of schoolboys.

The only difference as regarded the students was
that, instead of sitting under the pointer and listening
to the worn-out doctrines of a teacher, they practised
racing with five thousand horses; instead of the field
where they had played ball, they had the boundless
borderlands, where at the sight of them the Tatar
showed his keen face and the Turk frowned grimly
from under his green turban. The difference was that,
instead of being forced to the companionship of school,
they themselves had deserted their fathers and mothers
and fled from their homes; that here were those about
whose neck a rope had already been wound, and who,
instead of pale death, had seen life, and life in all its
intensity; those who, from generous habits, could
never keep a coin in their pockets; those who had
hitherto regarded a ducat as wealth, and whose pockets,
thanks to the Jew revenue-farmers, could have been
turned wrong side out without any danger of anything
falling from them. Here were students who could not
endure the academic rod, and had not carried away a
single letter from the schools; but with them were also
some who knew about Horace, Cicero, and the Roman
Republic. There were many leaders who afterwards

distinguished themselves in the king's armies; and there were numerous clever warriors who cherished a magnanimous conviction that it was of no consequence where they fought, so long as they did fight, since it was a disgrace to an honourable man to live without fighting. There were many who had come to the Setch for the sake of being able to say afterwards that they had been there and were therefore hardened warriors. But who was not there? This strange republic was a necessary outgrowth of the epoch. Lovers of a warlike life, of golden beakers and rich brocades, of ducats and gold pieces, could always find employment there. The lovers of women alone could find naught, for no woman dared show herself even in the suburbs of the Setch.

It seemed exceedingly strange to Ostap and Andríi that, although a crowd of people had come to the Setch with them, not a soul inquired, " Whence come these men? who are they? and what are their names? " They had come thither as though returning to a home whence they had departed only an hour before. The new-comer merely presented himself to the Koschevoi, or head chief of the Setch, who generally said, " Welcome! Do you believe in Christ? "—" I do," replied the new-comer. "And you believe in the Holy Trinity?" — " I do."—" And do you go to church? "—" I do." " Now cross yourself." The new-comer crossed himself. " Very good," replied the Koschevoi; " enter the kurén where you have most acquaintances." This concluded the ceremony. And all the Setch prayed in one church, and were willing to defend it to their last drop of blood, although they would not hearken to aught about fasting or abstinence. Jews, Armenians, and Tatars, inspired by strong avarice, took the liberty of living and trading in the suburbs; for the Zaporozhtzi never cared for bargaining, and paid whatever money their hand chanced to grasp in their pocket. Moreover, the lot of these gain-loving traders was pitiable in the extreme. They resembled people settled at the foot of Vesuvius; for when the Zaporozhtzi

lacked money, these bold adventurers broke down their
booths and took everything gratis. The Setch consisted
of over sixty kuréns, each of which greatly resembled
a separate independent republic, but still more a school
or seminary of children, always ready for anything.
No one had any occupation; no one retained anything
for himself; everything was in the hands of the hetman
of the kurén, who, on that account, generally bore the
title of "father." In his hands were deposited the
money, clothes, all the provisions, oatmeal, grain, even
the firewood. They gave him money to take care of.
Quarrels amongst the inhabitants of the kurén were
not unfrequent; and in such cases they proceeded at
once to blows. The inhabitants of the kurén swarmed
into the square, and smote each other with their fists,
until one side had finally gained the upper hand, when
the revelry began. Such was the Setch, which had such
an attraction for young men.

Ostap and Andríi flung themselves into this sea of
dissipation with all the ardour of youth, forgot in a trice
their father's house, the seminary, and all which had
hitherto exercised their minds, and gave themselves
wholly up to their new life. Everything interested them—
the jovial habits of the Setch, and its chaotic morals and
laws, which even seemed to them too strict for such a
free republic. If a Cossack stole the smallest trifle,
it was considered a disgrace to the whole Cossack community. He was bound to the pillar of shame, and a
club was laid beside him, with which each passer-by
was bound to deal him a blow until in this manner he
was beaten to death. He who did not pay his debts was
chained to a cannon, until some one of his comrades
should decide to ransom him by paying his debts for
him. But what made the deepest impression on Andríi
was the terrible punishment decreed for murder. A
hole was dug in his presence, the murderer was lowered
alive into it, and over him was placed a coffin containing
the body of the man he had killed, after which the
earth was thrown in upon both. Long afterwards the

fearful ceremony of this horrible execution haunted his mind, and the man who had been buried alive appeared to him with his terrible coffin.

Both the young Cossacks soon took a good standing among their fellows. They often sallied out upon the steppe with comrades from their kurén, and sometimes too with the whole kurén or with neighbouring kuréns, to shoot the innumerable steppe-birds of every sort, deer, and goats. Or they went out upon the lakes, the river, and its tributaries allotted to each kurén, to throw their nets and draw out rich prey for the enjoyment of the whole kurén. Although unversed in any trade exercised by a Cossack, they were soon remarked among the other youths for their obstinate bravery and daring in everything. Skilfully and accurately they fired at the mark, and swam the Dnieper against the current—a deed for which the novice was triumphantly received into the circle of Cossacks.

But old Taras was planning a different sphere of activity for them. Such an idle life was not to his mind; he wanted active employment. He reflected incessantly how to stir up the Setch to some bold enterprise, wherein a man could revel as became a warrior. At length he went one day to the Koschevoi, and said plainly:—

" Well, Koschevoi, it is time for the Zaporozhtzi to set out."

" There is nowhere for them to go," replied the Koschevoi, removing his short pipe from his mouth and spitting to one side.

" What do you mean by nowhere? We can go to Turkey or Tatary."

" Impossible to go either to Turkey or Tatary," replied the Koschevoi, putting his pipe coolly into his mouth again.

" Why impossible? "

" It is so; we have promised the Sultan peace."

" But he is a Mussulman; and God and the Holy Scriptures command us to slay Mussulmans."

" We have no right. If we had not sworn by our faith, it might be done; but now it is impossible."

" How is it impossible? How can you say that we have no right? Here are my two sons, both young men. Neither has been to war; and you say that we have no right, and that there is no need for the Zaporozhtzi to set out on an expedition."

" Well, it is not fitting."

" Then it must be fitting that Cossack strength should be wasted in vain, that a man should disappear like a dog without having done a single good deed, that he should be of no use to his country or to Christianity! Why, then, do we live? What the deuce do we live for? just tell me that. You are a sensible man, you were not chosen as Koschevoi without reason: so just tell me what we live for? "

The Koschevoi made no reply to this question. He was an obstinate Cossack. He was silent for a while, and then said, " Anyway, there will not be war."

" There will not be war? " Taras asked again.

" No."

" Then it is no use thinking about it? "

" It is not to be thought of."

" Wait, you devil's limb! " said Taras to himself: " you shall learn to know me! " and he at once resolved to have his revenge on the Koschevoi.

Having made an agreement with several others, he gave them liquor; and the drunken Cossacks staggered into the square, where on a post hung the kettledrums which were generally beaten to assemble the people. Not finding the sticks, which were kept by the drummer, they seized a piece of wood and began to beat. The first to respond to the drum-beat was the drummer, a tall man with but one eye, but a frightfully sleepy one for all that.

" Who dares to beat the drum? " he shouted.

" Hold your tongue! take your sticks, and beat when you are ordered! " replied the drunken men.

The drummer at once took from his pocket the sticks

which he had brought with him, well knowing the result
of such proceedings. The drum rattled, and soon black
swarms of Cossacks began to collect like bees in the
square. All formed in a ring; and at length, after the
third summons, the chiefs began to arrive—the Koschevoi with staff in hand, the symbol of his office; the
judge with the army-seal; the secretary with his ink-
bottle; and the osaul with his staff. The Koschevoi
and the chiefs took off their caps and bowed on all sides
to the Cossacks, who stood proudly with their arms
akimbo.

"What means this assemblage? what do you wish,
gentles?" said the Koschevoi. Shouts and exclama-
tions interrupted his speech.

"Resign your staff! resign your staff this moment,
you son of Satan! we will have you no longer!" shouted
some of the Cossacks in the crowd. Some of the sober
ones appeared to wish to oppose this, but both sober
and drunken fell to blows. The shouting and uproar
became universal.

The Koschevoi attempted to speak; but knowing
that the self-willed multitude, if enraged, might beat
him to death, as almost always happened in such cases,
he bowed very low, laid down his staff, and hid himself
in the crowd.

"Do you command us, gentles, to resign our insignia
of office?" said the judge, the secretary, and the osaul,
as they prepared to give up the ink-horn, army-seal, and
staff, upon the spot.

"No, you are to remain!" was shouted from the
crowd. "We only wanted to drive out the Koschevoi
because he is a woman, and we want a man for Koschevoi."

"Whom do you now elect as Koschevoi?" asked the
chiefs.

"We choose Kukubenko," shouted some.

"We won't have Kukubenko!" screamed another
party: "he is too young; the milk has not dried off
his lips yet."

" Let Schilo be hetman! " shouted some: " make Schilo our Koschevoi! "

" Away with your Schilo! " yelled the crowd; " what kind of a Cossack is he who is as thievish as a Tatar? To the devil in a sack with your drunken Schilo! "

" Borodaty! let us make Borodaty our Koschevoi! "

" We won't have Borodaty! To the evil one's mother with Borodaty! "

" Shout Kirdyaga! " whispered Taras Bulba to several.

" Kirdyaga, Kirdyaga! " shouted the crowd. " Borodaty, Borodaty! Kirdyaga, Kirdyaga! Schilo! Away with Schilo! Kirdyaga! "

All the candidates, on hearing their names mentioned, quitted the crowd, in order not to give any one a chance of supposing that they were personally assisting in their election.

" Kirdyaga, Kirdyaga! " echoed more strongly than the rest.

" Borodaty! "

They proceeded to decide the matter by a show of hands, and Kirdyaga won.

" Fetch Kirdyaga! " they shouted. Half a score of Cossacks immediately left the crowd—some of them hardly able to keep their feet, to such an extent had they drunk—and went directly to Kirdyaga to inform him of his election.

Kirdyaga, a very old but wise Cossack, had been sitting for some time in his kurén, as if he knew nothing of what was going on.

" What is it, gentles? What do you wish? " he inquired.

" Come, they have chosen you for Koschevoi."

" Have mercy, gentles! " said Kirdyaga. " How can I be worthy of such honour? Why should I be made Koschevoi? I have not sufficient capacity to fill such a post. Could no better person be found in all the army? "

" Come, I say! " shouted the Zaporozhtzi. Two of them seized him by the arms; and in spite of his plant-

ing his feet firmly they finally dragged him to the square,
accompanying his progress with shouts, blows from
behind with their fists, kicks, and exhortations. " Don't
hold back, you son of Satan! Accept the honour, you
dog, when it is given!" In this manner Kirdyaga was
conducted into the ring of Cossacks.

" How now, gentles? " announced those who had
brought him, " are you agreed that this Cossack shall
be your Koschevoi? "

" We are all agreed! " shouted the throng, and the
whole plain trembled for a long time afterwards from
the shout.

One of the chiefs took the staff and brought it to the
newly elected Koschevoi. Kirdyaga, in accordance with
custom, immediately refused it. The chief offered it a
second time; Kirdyaga again declined it, and then, at
the third offer, accepted the staff. A cry of approbation
rang out from the crowd, and again the whole plain
resounded afar with the Cossacks' shout. Then there
stepped out from among the people the four oldest of
them all, white-bearded, white-haired Cossacks; though
there were no very old men in the Setch, for none of the
Zaporozhtzi ever died in their beds. Taking each a
handful of earth, which recent rain had converted into
mud, they laid it on Kirdyaga's head. The wet earth
trickled down from his head on to his moustache and
cheeks and smeared his whole face. But Kirdyaga stood
immovable in his place, and thanked the Cossacks for
the honour shown him.

Thus ended the noisy election, concerning which we
cannot say whether it was as pleasing to the others as it
was to Bulba; by means of it he had revenged himself
on the former Koschevoi. Moreover, Kirdyaga was an
old comrade, and had been with him on the same
expeditions by sea and land, sharing the toils and hard-
ships of war. The crowd immediately dispersed to
celebrate the election, and such revelry ensued as Ostap
and Andrii had not yet beheld. The taverns were
attacked and mead, corn-brandy, and beer seized

without payment, the owners being only too glad to escape with whole skins themselves. The whole night passed amid shouts, songs, and rejoicings; and the rising moon gazed long at troops of musicians traversing the streets with guitars, flutes, tambourines, and the church choir, who were kept in the Setch to sing in church and glorify the deeds of the Zaporozhtzi. At length drunkenness and fatigue began to overpower even these strong heads, and here and there a Cossack could be seen to fall to the ground, embracing a comrade in fraternal fashion; whilst maudlin, and even weeping, the latter rolled upon the earth with him. Here a whole group would lie down in a heap; there a man would choose the most comfortable position and stretch himself out on a log of wood. The last, and strongest, still uttered some incoherent speeches; finally even they, yielding to the power of intoxication, flung themselves down and all the Setch slept.

IV

BUT next day Taras Bulba had a conference with the new Koschevoi as to the method of exciting the Cossacks to some enterprise. The Koschevoi, a shrewd and sensible Cossack, who knew the Zaporozhtzi thoroughly, said at first, " Oaths cannot be violated by any means "; but after a pause added, " No matter, it can be done. We will not violate them, but let us devise something. Let the people assemble, not at my summons, but of their own accord. You know how to manage that; and I will hasten to the square with the chiefs, as though we knew nothing about it."

Not an hour had elapsed after their conversation, when the drums again thundered. The drunken and senseless Cossacks assembled. A myriad Cossack caps were sprinkled over the square. A murmur arose, " Why? What? Why was the assembly beaten? "

No one answered. At length, in one quarter and another, it began to be rumoured about, "Behold, the Cossack strength is being vainly wasted: there is no war! Behold, our leaders have become as marmots, every one; their eyes swim in fat! Plainly, there is no justice in the world!" The other Cossacks listened at first, and then began themselves to say, " In truth, there is no justice in the world!" Their leaders seemed surprised at these utterances. Finally the Koschevoi stepped forward: " Permit me, Cossacks, to address you."

" Do so!"

" Touching the matter in question, gentles, none know better than yourselves that many Zaporozhtzi have run in debt to the Jew ale-house keepers and to their brethren, so that now they have not an atom of credit. Again, touching the matter in question, there are many young fellows who have no idea of what war is like, although you know, gentles, that without war a young man cannot exist. How make a Zaporozhetz out of him if he has never killed a Mussulman?"

" He speaks well," thought Bulba.

" Think not, however, gentles, that I speak thus in order to break the truce; God forbid! I merely mention it. Besides, it is a shame to see what sort of church we have for our God. Not only has the church remained without exterior decoration during all the years which by God's mercy the Setch has stood, but up to this day even the holy pictures have no adornments. No one has even thought of making them a silver frame; they have only received what some Cossacks have left them in their wills; and these gifts were poor, since they had drunk up nearly all they had during their lifetime. I am making you this speech, therefore, not in order to stir up a war against the Mussulmans; we have promised the Sultan peace, and it would be a great sin in us to break this promise, for we swore it on our law."

" What is he mixing things up like that for? " said Bulba to himself.

"So you see, gentles, that war cannot be begun; honour does not permit it. But according to my poor opinion, we might, I think, send out a few young men in boats and let them plunder the coasts of Anatolia a little. What do you think, gentles?"

"Lead us, lead us all!" shouted the crowd on all sides. "We are ready to lay down our lives for our faith."

The Koschevoi was alarmed. He by no means wished to stir up all Zaporozhe; a breach of the truce appeared to him on this occasion unsuitable. "Permit me, gentles, to address you further."

"Enough!" yelled the Cossacks; "you can say nothing better."

"If it must be so, then let it be so. I am the slave of your will. We know, and from Scripture too, that the voice of the people is the voice of God. It is impossible to devise anything better than the whole nation has devised. But here lies the difficulty; you know, gentles, that the Sultan will not permit that which delights our young men to go unpunished. We should be prepared at such a time, and our forces should be fresh, and then we should fear no one. But during their absence the Tatars may assemble fresh forces; the dogs do not show themselves in sight and dare not come while the master is at home, but they can bite his heels from behind, and bite painfully too. And if I must tell you the truth, we have not boats enough, nor powder ready in sufficient quantity, for all to go. But I am ready, if you please; I am the slave of your will."

The cunning hetman was silent. The various groups began to discuss the matter, and the hetmans of the kuréns to take counsel together; few were drunk fortunately, so they decided to listen to reason.

A number of men set out at once for the opposite shore of the Dnieper, to the treasury of the army, where in strict secrecy, under water and among the reeds, lay concealed the army chest and a portion of the arms captured from the enemy. Others hastened to inspect the boats and prepare them for service. In a twinkling the whole shore was thronged with men. Carpenters appeared with axes in their hands. Old, weather-beaten, broad-shouldered, strong-legged Zaporozhtzi, with black or silvered moustaches, rolled up their trousers, waded up to their knees in water, and dragged the boats on to the shore with stout ropes; others brought seasoned timber and all sorts of wood. The boats were freshly planked, turned bottom upwards, caulked and tarred, and then bound together side by side after Cossack fashion, with long strands of reeds, so that the swell of the waves might not sink them. Far along the shore they built fires and heated tar in copper cauldrons to smear the boats. The old and the experienced instructed the young. The blows and shouts of the workers rose all over the neighbourhood; the bank shook and moved about.

About this time a large ferry-boat began to near the shore. The mass of people standing in it began to wave their hands from a distance. They were Cossacks in torn, ragged gaberdines. Their disordered garments, for many had on nothing but their shirts, with a short pipe in their mouths, showed that they had either escaped from some disaster or had caroused to such an extent that they had drunk up all they had on their bodies. A short, broad-shouldered Cossack of about fifty stepped out from the midst of them and stood in front. He shouted and waved his hand more vigorously than any of the others; but his words could not be heard for the cries and hammering of the workmen.

" Whence come you? " asked the Koschevoi, as the boat touched the shore. All the workers paused in their labours, and, raising their axes and chisels, looked on expectantly.

" From a misfortune! " shouted the short Cossack.

" From what? "

" Permit me, noble Zaporozhtzi, to address you."

" Speak! "

" Or would you prefer to assemble a council? "

" Speak, we are all here."

The people all pressed together in one mass.

" Have you then heard nothing of what has been going on in the hetman's dominions? "

" What is it? " inquired one of the kurén hetmans.

" Eh! what! Evidently the Tatars have plastered up your ears so that you might hear nothing."

" Tell us then; what has been going on there? "

" That is going on the like of which no man born or christened ever yet has seen."

" Tell us what it is, you son of a dog! " shouted one of the crowd, apparently losing patience.

" Things have come to such a pass that our holy churches are no longer ours."

" How not ours? "

" They are pledged to the Jews. If the Jew is not first paid, there can be no mass."

" What are you saying? "

" And if the dog of a Jew does not make a sign with his unclean hand over the holy Easter-bread, it cannot be consecrated."

" He lies, brother gentles. It cannot be that an unclean Jew puts his mark upon the holy Easter-bread."

" Listen! I have not yet told all. Catholic priests are going about all over the Ukraine in carts. The harm lies not in the carts, but in the fact that not horses, but orthodox Christians,[1] are harnessed to them. Listen! I have not yet told all. They say that the Jewesses are making themselves petticoats out of our popes' vestments. Such are the deeds that are taking place in the Ukraine, gentles! And you sit here revelling in Zaporozhe; and evidently the Tatars have so scared you that you have no eyes, no ears, no anything, and know nothing that is going on in the world."

" Stop, stop! " broke in the Koschevoi, who up to that moment had stood with his eyes fixed upon the earth like all Zaporozhtzi, who, on important occasions,

[1] That is of the Greek Church. The Poles were Catholics.

never yielded to their first impulse, but kept silence, and meanwhile concentrated inwardly all the power of their indignation. " Stop! I also have a word to say. But what were you about? When your father the devil was raging thus, what were you doing yourselves? Had you no swords? How came you to permit such lawlessness? "

" Eh! how did we come to permit such lawlessness? You would have tried when there were fifty thousand of the Lyakhs [1] alone; yes, and it is a shame not to be concealed, when there are also dogs among us who have already accepted their faith."

" But your hetman and your leaders, what have they done? "

" God preserve any one from such deeds as our leaders performed! "

" How so? "

" Our hetman, roasted in a brazen ox, now lies in Warsaw; and the heads and hands of our leaders are being carried to all the fairs as a spectacle for the people. That is what our leaders did."

The whole throng became wildly excited. At first silence reigned all along the shore, like that which precedes a tempest; and then suddenly voices were raised and all the shore spoke:—

" What! The Jews hold the Christian churches in pledge! Roman Catholic priests have harnessed and beaten orthodox Christians! What! such torture has been permitted on Russian soil by the cursed unbelievers! And they have done such things to the leaders and the hetman? Nay, this shall not be, it shall not be." Such words came from all quarters. The Zaporozhtzi were moved, and knew their power. It was not the excitement of a giddy-minded folk. All who were thus agitated were strong, firm characters, not easily aroused, but, once aroused, preserving their inward heat long and obstinately. " Hang all the Jews! " rang through the crowd. " They shall not make petticoats for their

[1] Lyakhs, an opprobrious name for the Poles.

Jewesses out of popes' vestments! They shall not place their signs upon the holy wafers! Drown all the heathens in the Dnieper!" These words uttered by some one in the throng flashed like lightning through all minds, and the crowd flung themselves upon the suburb with the intention of cutting the throats of all the Jews.

The poor sons of Israel, losing all presence of mind, and not being in any case courageous, hid themselves in empty brandy-casks, in ovens, and even crawled under the skirts of their Jewesses; but the Cossacks found them wherever they were.

" Gracious nobles! " shrieked one Jew, tall and thin as a stick, thrusting his sorry visage, distorted with terror, from among a group of his comrades, " gracious nobles! suffer us to say a word, only one word. We will reveal to you what you never yet have heard, a thing more important than I can say—very important! "

" Well, say it," said Bulba, who always liked to hear what an accused man had to say.

" Gracious nobles," exclaimed the Jew, " such nobles were never seen, by heavens, never! Such good, kind, and brave men there never were in the world before! " His voice died away and quivered with fear. " How was it possible that we should think any evil of the Zaporozhtzi? Those men are not of us at all, those who have taken pledges in the Ukraine. By heavens, they are not of us! They are not Jews at all. The evil one alone knows what they are; they are only fit to be spat upon and cast aside. Behold, my brethren say the same! Is it not true, Schloma? is it not true, Schmul? "

" By heavens, it is true! " replied Schloma and Schmul, from among the crowd, both pale as clay, in their ragged caps.

" We never yet," continued the tall Jew, " have had any secret intercourse with your enemies, and we will have nothing to do with Catholics; may the evil one fly away with them! We are like own brothers to the Zaporozhtzi."

"What! the Zaporozhtzi are brothers to you!" exclaimed some one in the crowd. "Don't wait! the cursed Jews! Into the Dnieper with them, gentles! Drown all the unbelievers!"

These words were the signal. They seized the Jews by the arms and began to hurl them into the waves. Pitiful cries resounded on all sides; but the stern Zaporozhtzi only laughed when they saw the Jewish legs, cased in shoes and stockings, struggling in the air. The poor orator who had called down destruction upon himself jumped out of the caftan, by which they had seized him, and in his scant parti-coloured under waistcoat clasped Bulba's legs, and cried, in piteous tones, " Great lord! gracious noble! I knew your brother, the late Dóroscha. He was a warrior who was an ornament to all knighthood. I gave him eight hundred sequins when he was obliged to ransom himself from the Turks."

" You knew my brother?" asked Taras.

" By heavens, I knew him. He was a magnificent nobleman."

" And what is your name?"

" Yankel."

" Good," said Taras; and after reflecting, he turned to the Cossacks and spoke as follows: " There will always be plenty of time to hang the Jew, if it proves necessary; but for to-day give him to me."

So saying, Taras led him to his waggon, beside which stood his Cossacks. " Crawl under the waggon; lie down, and do not move. And you, brothers, do not surrender this Jew."

So saying, he returned to the square, for the whole crowd had long since collected there. All had at once abandoned the shore and the preparation of the boats; for a land-journey now awaited them, and not a sea-voyage, and they needed horses and waggons, not ships. All, both young and old, wanted to go on the expedition; and it was decided, on the advice of the chiefs, the hetmans of the kuréns, and the Koschevoi, and with the

approbation of the whole Zaporozhtzian army, to march
straight to Poland, to avenge the injury and disgrace
to their faith and to Cossack renown, to seize booty
from the cities, to burn villages and grain, and spread
their glory far over the steppe. All at once girded and
armed themselves. The Koschevoi grew a whole foot
taller. He was no longer the timid executor of the
restless wishes of a free people, but their untrammelled
master. He was a despot, who knew only to command.
All the independent and pleasure-loving warriors stood
in an orderly line, with respectfully bowed heads, not
venturing to raise their eyes, when the Koschevoi gave
his orders. He gave these quietly, without shouting
and without haste, but with pauses between, like an
experienced man deeply learned in Cossack affairs,
and carrying into execution, not for the first time, a
wisely matured enterprise.

" Examine yourselves, look well to yourselves;
examine all your equipments thoroughly," he said:
" put your teams and your tar-boxes [1] in order; test
your weapons. Take not many clothes with you: a
shirt and a couple of pairs of trousers to each Cossack,
and a pot of oatmeal and millet apiece—let no one take
any more. There will be plenty of provisions, all that
is needed, in the waggons. Let every Cossack have two
horses. And two hundred yoke of oxen must be taken,
for we shall require them at the fords and marshy
places. Keep order, gentles, above all things. I know
that there are some among you whom God has made
so greedy that they would like to tear up silk and
velvet for foot-cloths. Leave off such devilish habits;
reject all garments as plunder, and take only weapons:
though if valuables offer themselves, ducats or silver,
they are useful in any case. I tell you this beforehand,
gentles, if any one gets drunk on the expedition, he will
have a short shrift: I will have him dragged by the
neck like a dog behind the baggage waggons, no matter

[1] The Cossack waggons have their axles smeared with tar
instead of grease.

who he may be, even were he the most heroic Cossack
in the whole army; he shall be shot on the spot like a
dog, and flung out, without sepulture, to be torn by the
birds of prey, for a drunkard on the march deserves
no Christian burial. Young men, obey the old men in
all things! If a ball grazes you, or a sword cuts your
head or any other part, attach no importance to such
trifles. Mix a charge of powder in a cup of brandy,
quaff it heartily, and all will pass off—you will not
even have any fever; and if the wound is large, put
simple earth upon it, mixing it first with spittle in your
palm, and that will dry it up. And now to work, to work,
lads, and look well to all, and without haste."

So spoke the Koschevoi; and no sooner had he
finished his speech than all the Cossacks at once set to
work. All the Setch grew sober. Nowhere was a single
drunken man to be found, it was as though there never
had been such a thing among the Cossacks. Some
attended to the tyres of the wheels, others changed the
axles of the waggons; some carried sacks of provisions
to them or loaded them with arms; others again drove
up the horses and oxen. On all sides resounded the
tramp of horses' hoofs, test-shots from the guns, the
clank of swords, the lowing of oxen, the screech of
rolling waggons, talking, sharp cries and urging-on of
cattle. Soon the Cossack force spread far over all the
plain; and he who might have undertaken to run from
its van to its rear would have had a long course. In the
little wooden church the priest was offering up prayers
and sprinkling all worshippers with holy water. All
kissed the cross. When the camp broke up and the
army moved out of the Setch, all the Zaporozhtzi
turned their heads back. "Farewell, our mother!"
they said almost in one breath. "May God preserve
thee from all misfortune!"

As he passed through the suburb, Taras Bulba saw
that his Jew, Yankel, had already erected a sort of
booth with an awning, and was selling flints, screw-
drivers, powder, and all sorts of military stores needed

on the road, even to rolls and bread. " What devils
these Jews are! " thought Taras; and riding up to
him, he said, " Fool, why are you sitting here? do you
want to be shot like a crow? "

Yankel in reply approached nearer, and making a
sign with both hands, as though wishing to impart some
secret, said, " Let the noble lord but keep silence and
say nothing to any one. Among the Cossack waggons
is a waggon of mine. I am carrying all sorts of needful
stores for the Cossacks, and on the journey I will furnish
every sort of provisions at a lower price than any Jew
ever sold at before. 'Tis so, by heavens! by heavens,
'tis so! "

Taras Bulba shrugged his shoulders in amazement at
the Jewish nature, and went on to the camp.

V

ALL South-west Poland speedily became a prey to fear.
Everywhere the rumour flew, " The Zaporozhtzi! the
Zaporozhtzi have appeared! " All who could flee did
so. All rose and scattered after the manner of that
lawless, reckless age, when they built neither fortresses
nor castles, but each man erected a temporary dwelling
of straw wherever he happened to find himself. He
thought, " It is useless to waste money and labour on
an izbá, when the roving Tatars will carry it off in any
case." All was in an uproar: one exchanged his plough
and oxen for a horse and gun, and joined an armed
band; another, seeking concealment, drove off his
cattle and carried off all the household stuff he could.
Occasionally, on the road, some were encountered who
met their visitors with arms in their hands; but the
majority fled before their arrival. All knew that it was
hard to deal with the raging and warlike throng known
by the name of the Zaporozhian army; a body which
under its independent and disorderly exterior, concealed

an organisation well calculated for times of battle. The horsemen rode steadily on without overburdening or heating their horses; the foot-soldiers marched quietly behind the waggons; and the whole force moved only by night, resting during the day, and selecting for this purpose desert tracts, uninhabited spots, and forests, of which there were then plenty. Spies and scouts were sent ahead to study the time, place, and method of attack. And lo! the Zaporozhtzi suddenly appeared in those places where they were least expected: then all were put to the sword; the villages were burned; and the horses and cattle which were not driven off behind the army killed upon the spot. They seemed to be fiercely revelling, rather than carrying out a military expedition. Our hair would stand on end nowadays at the horrible traits of that fierce, half-civilised age, which the Zaporozhtzi everywhere exhibited: children killed, women's breasts cut open, the skin flayed from the legs up to the knees, and the victim then set at liberty. In short, the Cossacks paid their former debts in coin of full weight. The abbot of one monastery, on hearing of their approach, sent two monks to say that they were not behaving as they should; that there was an agreement between the Zaporozhtzi and the government; that they were breaking faith with the king, and violating all international rights. " Tell your bishop from me and from all the Zaporozhtzi," said the Koschevoi, " that he has nothing to fear: the Cossacks, so far, have only lighted and smoked their pipes." And the magnificent abbey was soon wrapped in the devouring flames, its tall Gothic windows showing grimly through the waves of fire as they parted. The fleeing mass of monks, women, and Jews thronged into those towns where any hope lay in the garrison and the civic forces. The aid sent in season by the government, but delayed on the way, consisted of a few troops which either were unable to enter the towns or, seized with fright, turned their backs at the very first en-counter and fled on their swift horses. However, several of the royal commanders, who had conquered in former battles, resolved to unite their forces and confront the Zaporozhtzi.

And here, above all, did our young Cossacks, disgusted with pillage, greed, and a feeble foe, and burning with the desire to distinguish themselves in presence of their chiefs, seek to measure themselves in single combat with the warlike and boastful Lyakhs, prancing on their spirited horses, with the sleeves of their jackets thrown back and streaming in the wind. This game was inspiriting: they won at it many costly sets of horse-trappings and valuable weapons. In a month the scarcely fledged birds attained their full growth, were completely transformed, and became men; their features, in which hitherto a trace of youthful softness had been visible, grew strong and grim. But it was pleasant to old Taras to see his sons among the foremost. It seemed as though Ostap were designed by nature for the game of war and the difficult science of command. Never once losing his head or becoming confused under any circumstances, he could, with a cool audacity almost supernatural in a youth of two-and-twenty, in an instant gauge the danger and the whole scope of the matter, could at once devise a means of escaping, but of escaping only that he might the more surely conquer. His movements now began to be marked by the assurance which comes from experience, and in them could be detected the germ of the future leader. His person strengthened, and his bearing grew majestically leonine. " What a fine leader he will make one of these days! " said old Taras. " He will make a splendid leader, far surpassing even his father! "

Andríi gave himself up wholly to the enchanting music of blades and bullets. He knew not what it was to consider, or calculate, or to measure his own as against the enemy's strength. He gazed on battle with mad delight and intoxication: he found something festal in the moments when a man's brain burns, when all things wave and flutter before his eyes, when heads are stricken off, horses fall to the earth with a sound of thunder, and he rides on like a drunken man, amid the whistling of bullets and the flashing of swords, dealing blows to all, and heeding not those aimed at himself. More than once their father marvelled too at Andríi, seeing him, stirred only by a flash of impulse, dash at something which a sensible man in cold blood never would have attempted, and, by the sheer force of his mad attack, accomplish such wonders as could not but amaze even men grown old in battle. Old Taras admired and said, " And he too will make a good warrior if the enemy does not capture him meanwhile. He is not Ostap, but he is a dashing warrior, nevertheless."

The army decided to march straight on the city of Dubno, which, rumour said, contained much wealth and many rich inhabitants. The journey was accomplished in a day and a half, and the Zaporozhtzi appeared before the city. The inhabitants resolved to defend themselves to the utmost extent of their power, and to fight to the last extremity, preferring to die in their squares and streets, and on their thresholds, rather than admit the enemy to their houses. A high rampart of earth surrounded the city; and in places where it was low or weak, it was strengthened by a wall of stone, or a house which served as a redoubt, or even an oaken stockade. The garrison was strong and aware of the importance of their position. The Zaporozhtzi attacked the wall fiercely, but were met by a shower of grape-shot. The citizens and residents of the town evidently did not wish to remain idle, but gathered on the ramparts; in their eyes could be read desperate resistance. The women too were determined to take part in the fray, and upon the heads of the Zaporozhians rained down stones, casks of boiling water, and sacks of lime which blinded them. The Zaporozhtzi were not fond of having anything to do with fortified places: sieges were not in their line. The Koschevoi ordered them to retreat, saying, " It is useless, brother gentles; we will retire: but may I be a heathen Tatar, and not a

Christian, if we do not clear them out of that town!
may they all perish of hunger, the dogs! " The army
retreated, surrounded the town, and, for lack of something to do, busied themselves with devastating the
surrounding country, burning the neighbouring villages
and the ricks of unthreshed grain, and turning their
droves of horses loose in the cornfields, as yet untouched
by the reaping-hook, where the plump ears waved,
fruit, as luck would have it, of an unusually good harvest
which should have liberally rewarded all tillers of the
soil that season.

With horror those in the city beheld their means of
subsistence destroyed. Meanwhile the Zaporozhtzi,
having formed a double ring of their waggons around
the city, disposed themselves as in the Setch in kuréns,
smoked their pipes, bartered their booty for weapons,
played at leapfrog and odd-and-even, and gazed at
the city with deadly cold-bloodedness. At night they
lighted their camp-fires, and the cooks boiled the
porridge for each kurén in huge copper cauldrons;
whilst an alert sentinel watched all night beside
the blazing fire. But the Zaporozhtzi soon began
to tire of inactivity and prolonged sobriety, unaccom-
panied by any fighting. The Koschevoi even ordered
the allowance of wine to be doubled, which was sometimes done in the army when no difficult enterprises or
movements were on hand. The young men, and Taras
Bulba's sons in particular, did not like this life. Andríi
was visibly bored. " You silly fellow! " said Taras to
him, " be patient, you will be hetman one day. He is
not a good warrior who loses heart in an important
enterprise; but he who is not tired even of inactivity,
who endures all, and who even if he likes a thing can
give it up." But hot youth cannot agree with age:
the two have different natures, and look at the same
thing with different eyes.

But in the meantime Taras's band, led by Tovkatch,
arrived; with him were also two osauls, the secretary,
and other regimental officers: the Cossacks numbered

over four thousand in all. There were among them many
volunteers, who had risen of their own free will, without
any summons, as soon as they heard what the matter
was. The osauls brought to Taras's sons the blessing
of their aged mother, and to each a picture in a cypress-
wood frame from the Mezhigorski monastery at Kief.
The two brothers hung the pictures round their necks,
and involuntarily grew pensive as they remembered
their old mother. What did this blessing prophesy?
Was it a blessing for their victory over the enemy, and
then a joyous return to their home with booty and
glory, to be everlastingly commemorated in the songs
of guitar-players? or was it . . .? But the future is
unknown, and stands before a man like autumnal fogs
rising from the swamps; birds fly foolishly up and
down in it with flapping wings, never recognising each
other, the dove seeing not the vulture, nor the vulture
the dove, and no one knowing how far he may be flying
from destruction.

Ostap had long since attended to his duties and gone
to the kurén. Andríi, without knowing why, felt a kind
of oppression at his heart. The Cossacks had finished
their evening meal; the wonderful July night had completely fallen; still he did not go to the kurén, nor lie
down to sleep, but gazed unconsciously at the whole
scene before him. In the sky innumerable stars twinkled
brightly. The plain was covered far and wide with
scattered waggons with swinging tar-buckets, smeared
with tar, and loaded with every description of goods
and provisions captured from the foe. Beside the
waggons, under the waggons, and far beyond the
waggons, Zaporozhtzi were everywhere visible, stretched
upon the grass. They all slumbered in picturesque
attitudes; one had thrust a sack under his head,
another his cap, and another simply made use of his
comrade's side. Swords, guns, matchlocks, short pipe-
stems with copper mountings, iron awls, and a flint and
steel were inseparable from every Cossack. The heavy
oxen lay with their feet doubled under them like huge

whitish masses, and at a distance looked like grey stones scattered on the slopes of the plain. On all sides the heavy snores of sleeping warriors began to arise from the grass, and were answered from the plain by the ringing neighs of their steeds, chafing at their hobbled feet. Meanwhile a certain threatening magnificence had mingled with the beauty of the July night. It was the distant glare of the burning district afar. In one place the flames spread quietly and grandly over the sky; in another, suddenly bursting into a whirl-wind, they hissed and flew upwards to the very stars, and floating fragments died away in the most distant quarter of the heavens. Here the black, burned monas-tery like a grim Carthusian monk stood threatening, and displaying its dark magnificence at every flash; there blazed the monastery garden. It seemed as though the trees could be heard hissing as they stood wrapped in smoke; and when the fire burst forth, it suddenly lighted up the ripe plums with a phosphoric lilac-coloured gleam, or turned the yellowing pears here and there to pure gold. In the midst of them hung black against the wall of the building, or the trunk of a tree, the body of some poor Jew or monk who had perished in the flames with the structure. Above the distant fires hovered a flock of birds, like a cluster of tiny black crosses upon a fiery field. The town thus laid bare seemed to sleep; the spires and roofs, and its palisade and walls, gleamed quietly in the glare of the distant conflagrations. Andríi went the rounds of the Cossack ranks. The camp-fires, beside which the sen-tinels sat, were ready to go out at any moment; and even the sentinels slept, having devoured oatmeal and dumplings with true Cossack appetites. He was aston-ished at such carelessness, thinking, " It is well that there is no strong enemy at hand and nothing to fear." Finally he went to one of the waggons, climbed into it, and lay down upon his back, putting his clasped hands under his head; but he could not sleep, and gazed long at the sky. It was all open before him; the air was pure and transparent; the dense clusters of stars in the Milky Way, crossing the sky like a belt, were flooded with light. From time to time Andríi in some degree lost consciousness, and a light mist of dream veiled the heavens from him for a moment; but then he awoke, and they became visible again.

During one of these intervals it seemed to him that some strange human figure flitted before him. Thinking it to be merely a vision which would vanish at once, he opened his eyes, and beheld a withered, emaciated face bending over him, and gazing straight into his own. Long coal-black hair, unkempt, dishevelled, fell from beneath a dark veil which had been thrown over the head; whilst the strange gleam of the eyes, and the death-like tone of the sharp-cut features, inclined him to think that it was an apparition. His hand involuntarily grasped his gun; and he exclaimed almost convulsively: "Who are you? If you are an evil spirit, avaunt! If you are a living being, you have chosen an ill time for your jest. I will kill you with one shot."

In answer to this, the apparition laid its finger upon its lips and seemed to entreat silence. He dropped his hand and began to look more attentively. He recognised it to be a woman from the long hair, the brown neck, and the half-concealed bosom. But she was not a native of those regions: her wide cheek-bones stood out prominently over her hollow cheeks; her small eyes were obliquely set. The more he gazed at her features, the more he found them familiar. Finally he could restrain himself no longer, and said, "Tell me, who are you? It seems to me that I know you, or have seen you somewhere."

"Two years ago in Kief."

"Two years ago in Kief!" repeated Andríi, endeavouring to collect in his mind all that lingered in his memory of his former student life. He looked intently at her once more, and suddenly exclaimed at the top of his voice, "You are the Tatar! the servant of the lady, the Waiwode's daughter!"

" Sh! " cried the Tatar, clasping her hands with a supplicating glance, trembling all over, and turning her head round in order to see whether any one had been awakened by Andríi's loud exclamation.

" Tell me, tell me, why are you here? " said Andríi almost breathlessly, in a whisper, interrupted every moment by inward emotion. " Where is the lady? is she alive? "

" She is now in the city."

" In the city! " he exclaimed, again almost in a shriek, and feeling all the blood suddenly rush to his heart. " Why is she in the city? "

" Because the old lord himself is in the city: he has been Waiwode of Dubno for the last year and a half."

" Is she married? How strange you are! Tell me about her."

" She has eaten nothing for two days."

" What! "

" And not one of the inhabitants has had a morsel of bread for a long while; all have long been eating earth."

Andríi was astounded.

" The lady saw you from the city wall, among the Zaporozhtzi. She said to me, ' Go tell the warrior: if he remembers me, let him come to me; and do not forget to make him give you a bit of bread for my aged mother, for I do not wish to see my mother die before my very eyes. Better that I should die first, and she afterwards! Beseech him; clasp his knees, his feet: he also has an aged mother, let him give you the bread for her sake! ' "

Many feelings awoke in the young Cossack's breast.

" But how came you here? how did you get here? "

" By an underground passage."

" Is there an underground passage? "

" Yes."

" Where? "

" You will not betray it, warrior? "

" I swear it by the holy cross! "

" You descend into a hole, and cross the brook, yonder among the reeds."

" And it leads into the city? "

" Straight into the monastery."

" Let us go, let us go at once."

" A bit of bread, in the name of Christ and of His holy mother! "

" Good, so be it. Stand here beside the waggon, or, better still, lie down in it: no one will see you, all are asleep. I will return at once."

And he set off for the baggage waggons, which contained the provisions belonging to their kurén. His heart beat. All the past, all that had been extinguished by the Cossack bivouacks, and by the stern battle of life, flamed out at once on the surface and drowned the present in its turn. Again, as from the dark depths of the sea, the noble lady rose before him: again there gleamed in his memory her beautiful arms, her eyes, her laughing mouth, her thick dark-chestnut hair, falling in curls upon her shoulders, and the firm, well-rounded limbs of her maiden form. No, they had not been extinguished in his breast, they had not vanished, they had simply been laid aside, in order, for a time, to make way for other strong emotions; but often, very often, the young Cossack's deep slumber had been troubled by them, and often he had lain sleepless on his couch, without being able to explain the cause.

His heart beat more violently at the thought of seeing her again, and his young knees shook. On reaching the baggage waggons, he had quite forgotten what he had come for; he raised his hand to his brow and rubbed it long, trying to recollect what he was to do. At length he shuddered, and was filled with terror as the thought suddenly occurred to him that she was dying of hunger. He jumped upon the waggon and seized several large loaves of black bread; but then he thought, " Is this not food, suited to a robust and easily satisfied Zaporozhetz, too coarse and unfit for her delicate frame? " Then he recollected that the Koschevoi, on the previous

evening, had reproved the cooks for having cooked up
all the oatmeal into porridge at once, when there was
plenty for three times. Sure that he would find
plenty of porridge in the kettles, he drew out his
father's travelling kettle and went with it to the cook
of their kurén, who was sleeping beside two big cauldrons, holding about ten pailfuls, under which the ashes
still glowed. Glancing into them, he was amazed to find
them empty. It must have required supernatural powers
to eat it all; the more so, as their kurén numbered
fewer than the others. He looked into the cauldron
of the other kuréns — nothing anywhere. Involuntarily the saying recurred to his mind, " The Zaporozhtzi
are like children: if there is little they eat it, if there
is much they leave nothing." What was to be done?
There was, somewhere in the waggon belonging to his
father's band, a sack of white bread, which they had
found when they pillaged the bakery of the monastery.
He went straight to his father's waggon, but it was not
there. Ostap had taken it and put it under his head;
and there he lay, stretched on the ground, snoring so
that the whole plain rang again. Andríi seized the sack
abruptly with one hand and gave it a jerk, so that
Ostap's head fell to the ground. The elder brother
sprang up in his sleep, and, sitting there with closed
eyes, shouted at the top of his lungs, " Stop them!
Stop the cursed Lyakhs! Catch the horses! catch the
horses! "—" Silence! I'll kill you," shouted Andríi in
terror, flourishing the sack over him. But Ostap did
not continue his speech, sank down again, and gave
such a snore that the grass on which he lay waved with
his breath.

Andríi glanced timidly on all sides to see if Ostap's
talking in his sleep had waked any of the Cossacks.
Only one long-locked head was raised in the adjoining
kurén, and after glancing about, was dropped back on
the ground. After waiting a couple of minutes he set
out with his load. The Tatar woman was lying where
he had left her, scarcely breathing. " Come, rise up.

Fear not, all are sleeping. Can you take one of these loaves if I cannot carry all? " So saying, he swung the sack on to his back, pulled out another sack of millet as he passed the waggon, took in his hands the loaves he had wanted to give the Tatar woman to carry, and, bending somewhat under the load, went boldly through the ranks of sleeping Zaporozhtzi.

" Andríi," said old Bulba, as he passed. His heart died within him. He halted, trembling, and said softly, " What is it? "

" There's a woman with you. When I get up I'll give you a sound thrashing. Women will lead you to no good." So saying, he leaned his head upon his hand and gazed intently at the muffled form of the Tatar.

Andríi stood there, more dead than alive, not daring to look in his father's face. When he did raise his eyes and glance at him, old Bulba was asleep, with his head still resting in the palm of his hand.

Andríi crossed himself. Fear fled from his heart even more rapidly than it had assailed it. When he turned to look at the Tatar woman, she stood before him, muffled in her mantle, like a dark granite statue, and the gleam of the distant dawn lighted up only her eyes, dull as those of a corpse. He plucked her by the sleeve, and both went on together, glancing back continually. At length they descended the slope of a small ravine, almost a hole, along the bottom of which a brook flowed lazily, overgrown with sedge, and strewed with mossy boulders. Descending into this ravine, they were completely concealed from the view of all the plain occupied by the Zaporovian camp. At least Andríi, glancing back, saw that the steep slope rose behind him higher than a man. On its summit appeared a few blades of steppe-grass; and behind them, in the sky, hung the moon, like a golden sickle. The breeze rising on the steppe warned them that the dawn was not far off. But nowhere was the crow of the cock heard. Neither in the city nor in the devastated neighbourhood had there been a cock for a long time past. They crossed the brook on a small plank, beyond which rose the opposite bank, which appeared higher than the one behind them and rose steeply. It seemed as though this were the strong point of the citadel upon which the besieged could rely; at all events, the earthen wall was lower there, and no garrison appeared behind it. But farther on rose the thick monastery walls. The steep bank was overgrown with steppe-grass, and in the narrow ravine between it and the brook grew tall reeds almost as high as a man. At the summit of the bank were the remains of a wattled fence, which had formerly surrounded some garden, and in front of it were visible the wide leaves of the burdock, from among which rose blackthorn, and sunflowers lifting their heads high above all the rest. Here the Tatar flung off her slippers and went barefoot, gathering her clothes up carefully, for the spot was marshy and full of water. Forcing their way among the reeds, they stopped before a ruined outwork. Skirting this outwork, they found a sort of earthen arch—an opening not much larger than the opening of an oven. The Tatar woman bent her head and went first. Andríi followed, bending as low as he could, in order to pass with his sacks; and both soon found themselves in total darkness.

VI

ANDRÍI could hardly move in the dark and narrow earthen burrow, as he followed the Tatar, dragging after him his sacks of bread. " It will soon be light," said his guide: " we are approaching the spot where I placed a light." And in fact the dark earthen walls began to be gradually lit up. They reached a widening in the passage where, it seemed, there had once been a chapel; at least, there was a small table against the wall, like an altar, and above, the faded, almost entirely obliterated picture of a Catholic Madonna. A small silver lamp hanging before it barely illumined it.

The Tatar stooped and picked up from the ground a copper candlestick which she had left there, a candlestick with a tall, slender stem, and snuffers, pin, and extinguisher hanging about it on chains. She lighted it at the silver lamp. The light grew stronger; and as they went on, now illumined by it, and again enveloped in pitchy shadow, they suggested a picture by Gerard Dow.

The warrior's fresh, handsome countenance, overflowing with health and youth, presented a strong contrast to the pale, emaciated face of his companion. The passage grew a little higher, so that Andríi could hold himself erect. He gazed with curiosity at the earthen walls. Here and there, as in the catacombs at Kief, were niches in the walls; and in some places coffins were standing. Sometimes they came across human bones which had become softened with the dampness and were crumbling into dust. It was evident that pious folk had taken refuge here from the storms, sorrows, and seductions of the world. It was extremely damp in some places; indeed there was water under their feet at intervals. Andríi was forced to halt frequently to allow his companion to rest, for her fatigue kept increasing. The small piece of bread she had swallowed only caused a pain in her stomach, of late unused to food; and she often stood motionless for minutes together in one spot.

At length a small iron door appeared before them. " Glory be to God, we have arrived! " said the Tatar in a faint voice, and tried to lift her hand to knock, but had no strength to do so. Andríi knocked hard at the door in her stead. There was an echo as though a large space lay beyond the door; then the echo changed as if resounding through lofty arches. In a couple of minutes, keys rattled, and steps were heard descending some stairs. At length the door opened, and a monk, standing on the narrow stairs with the key and a light in his hands, admitted them. Andríi involuntarily halted at the sight of a Catholic monk—one of those

who had aroused such hate and disdain among the
Cossacks that they treated them even more inhumanly
than they treated the Jews.

The monk, on his part, started back on perceiving a
Zaporovian Cossack, but a whisper from the Tatar
reassured him. He lighted them in, fastened the door
behind them, and led them up the stairs. They found
themselves beneath the dark and lofty arches of the
monastery church. Before one of the altars, adorned
with tall candlesticks and candles, knelt a priest praying
quietly. Near him on each side knelt two young choris-
ters in lilac cassocks and white lace stoles, with censers
in their hands. He prayed for the performance of a
miracle, that the city might be saved; that their souls
might be strengthened; that patience might be given
them; that doubt and timid, weak-spirited mourning
over earthly misfortunes might be banished. A few
women, resembling shadows, knelt supporting themselves against the backs of the chairs and dark wooden
benches before them, and laying their exhausted heads
upon them. A few men stood sadly, leaning against the
columns upon which the wide arches rested. The
stained-glass window above the altar suddenly glowed
with the rosy light of dawn; and from it, on the floor,
fell circles of blue, yellow, and other colours, illuminat-
ing the dim church. The whole altar was lighted up;
the smoke from the censers hung a cloudy rainbow in
the air. Andríi gazed from his dark corner, not without
surprise, at the wonders worked by the light. At that
moment the magnificent swell of the organ filled the
whole church. It grew deeper and deeper, expanded,
swelled into heavy bursts of thunder; and then all at
once, turning into heavenly music, its ringing tones
floated high among the arches, like clear maiden voices,
and again descended into a deep roar and thunder, and
then ceased. The thunderous pulsations echoed long
and tremulously among the arches; and Andríi, with
half-open mouth, admired the wondrous music.

Then he felt some one plucking the skirt of his caftan.

" It is time," said the Tatar. They traversed the
church unperceived, and emerged upon the square in
front. Dawn had long flushed the heavens; all announced sunrise. The square was empty: in the middle
of it still stood wooden pillars, showing that, perhaps
only a week before, there had been a market here
stocked with provisions. The streets, which were
unpaved, were simply a mass of dried mud. The square
was surrounded by small, one-storied stone or mud
houses, in the walls of which were visible wooden stakes
and posts obliquely crossed by carved wooden beams,
as was the manner of building in those days. Specimens
of it can still be seen in some parts of Lithuania and
Poland. They were all covered with enormously high
roofs, with a multitude of windows and air-holes. On
one side, close to the church, rose a building quite
detached from and taller than the rest, probably the
town-hall or some official structure. It was two stories
high, and above it, on two arches, rose a belvedere where
a watchman stood; a huge clock-face was let into the
roof.

The square seemed deserted, but Andríi thought he
heard a feeble groan. Looking about him, he perceived,
on the farther side, a group of two or three men lying
motionless upon the ground. He fixed his eyes more
intently on them, to see whether they were asleep or
dead; and, at the same moment, stumbled over something lying at his feet. It was the dead body of a
woman, a Jewess apparently. She appeared to be young,
though this was scarcely discernible in her distorted
and emaciated features. Upon her head was a red silk
kerchief; two rows of pearls or pearl beads adorned
the earpieces of her head-dress, from beneath which
two long curls hung down upon her shrivelled neck,
with its tightly drawn veins. Beside her lay a child,
grasping convulsively at her shrunken breast, and
squeezing it with involuntary ferocity at finding no
milk there. He neither wept nor screamed, and only his
gently rising and falling body would have led one to

guess that he was not dead, or at least on the point of breathing his last. They turned into a street, and were suddenly stopped by a madman, who, catching sight of Andríi's precious burden, sprang upon him like a tiger, and clutched him, yelling, " Bread! " But his strength was not equal to his madness. Andríi repulsed him and he fell to the ground. Moved with pity, the young Cossack flung him a loaf, which he seized like a mad dog, gnawing and biting it; but nevertheless he shortly expired in horrible suffering, there in the street, from the effect of long abstinence. The ghastly victims of hunger startled them at every step. Many, apparently unable to endure their torments in their houses, seemed to run into the streets to see whether some nourishing power might not possibly descend from the air. At the gate of one house sat an old woman, and it was impossible to say whether she was asleep or dead, or only unconscious; at all events, she no longer saw or heard anything, and sat immovable in one spot, her head drooping on her breast. From the roof of another house hung a worn and wasted body in a rope noose. The poor fellow could not endure the tortures of hunger to the last, and had preferred to hasten his end by a voluntary death.

At the sight of such terrible proofs of famine, Andríi could not refrain from saying to the Tatar, " Is there really nothing with which they can prolong life? If a man is driven to extremities, he must feed on what he has hitherto despised; he can sustain himself with creatures which are forbidden by the law. Anything can be eaten under such circumstances."

" They have eaten everything," said the Tatar, " all the animals. Not a horse, nor a dog, nor even a mouse is to be found in the whole city. We never had any store of provisions in the town: they were all brought from the villages."

" But how can you, while dying such a fearful death, still dream of defending the city? "

" Possibly the Waiwode might have surrendered; but

yesterday morning the commander of the troops at
Buzhana sent a hawk into the city with a note saying
that it was not to be given up; that he was coming to
its rescue with his forces, and was only waiting for
another leader, that they might march together. And
now they are expected every moment. But we have
reached the house.''

Andríi had already noticed from a distance this house,
unlike the others, and built apparently by some Italian
architect. It was constructed of thin red bricks, and
had two stories. The windows of the lower story were
sheltered under lofty, projecting granite cornices. The
upper story consisted entirely of small arches, forming
a gallery; between the arches were iron gratings enriched
with escutcheons; whilst upon the gables of the house
more coats-of-arms were displayed. The broad external
staircase, of tinted bricks, abutted on the square. At
the foot of it sat guards, who with one hand held their
halberds upright, and with the other supported their
drooping heads, and in this attitude more resembled
apparitions than living beings. They neither slept nor
dreamed, but seemed quite insensible to everything;
they even paid no attention to who went up the stairs.
At the head of the stairs, they found a richly-dressed
warrior, armed cap-à-pie, and holding a breviary in his
hand. He turned his dim eyes upon them; but the
Tatar spoke a word to him, and he dropped them again
upon the open pages of his breviary. They entered the
first chamber, a large one, serving either as a reception-
room, or simply as an ante-room; it was filled with
soldiers, servants, secretaries, huntsmen, cup-bearers,
and the other servitors indispensable to the support of
a Polish magnate's state, all seated along the walls.
The reek of extinguished candles was perceptible; and
two were still burning in two huge candlesticks, nearly
as tall as a man, standing in the middle of the room,
although morning had long since peeped through the
wide grated window. Andríi wanted to go straight on
to the large oaken door adorned with a coat-of-arms

and a profusion of carved ornaments, but the Tatar
pulled his sleeve and pointed to a small door in the side
wall. Through this they gained a corridor, and then a
room, which he began to examine attentively. The
light which filtered through a crack in the shutters
fell upon several objects—a crimson curtain, a gilded
cornice, and a painting on the wall. Here the Tatar
motioned to Andríi to wait, and opened the door into
another room from which flashed the light of a fire. He
heard a whispering, and a soft voice which made him
quiver all over. Through the open door he saw flit
rapidly past a tall female figure, with a long thick braid
of hair falling over her uplifted hands. The Tatar
returned and told him to go in.

He could never understand how he entered and how
the door was shut behind him. Two candles burned
in the room and a lamp glowed before the images:
beneath the lamp stood a tall table with steps to kneel
upon during prayer, after the Catholic fashion. But his
eye did not seek this. He turned to the other side and
perceived a woman, who appeared to have been frozen
or turned to stone in the midst of some quick movement.
It seemed as though her whole form had sought to
spring towards him, and had suddenly paused. And he
stood in like manner amazed before her. Not thus had
he pictured to himself that he should find her. This was
not the same being he had formerly known; nothing
about her resembled her former self; but she was twice
as beautiful, twice as enchanting, now than she had been
then. Then there had been something unfinished, incom-
plete, about her; now here was a production to which the
artist had given the finishing stroke of his brush. That
was a charming, giddy girl; this was a woman in the
full development of her charms. As she raised her eyes,
they were full of feeling, not of mere hints of feeling.
The tears were not yet dry in them, and framed them
in a shining dew which penetrated the very soul. Her
bosom, neck, and arms were moulded in the proportions
which mark fully developed loveliness. Her hair, which

had in former days waved in light ringlets about her face, had become a heavy. luxuriant mass, a part of which was caught up, while part fell in long, slender curls upon her arms and breast. It seemed as though her every feature had changed. In vain did he seek to discover in them a single one of those which were engraved in his memory—a single one. Even her great pallor did not lessen her wonderful beauty; on the contrary, it conferred upon it an irresistible, inexpressible charm. Andríi felt in his heart a noble timidity, and stood motionless before her. She, too, seemed surprised at the appearance of the Cossack, as he stood before her in all the beauty and might of his young manhood, and in the very immovability of his limbs personified the utmost freedom of movement. His eyes beamed with clear decision; his velvet brows curved in a bold arch; his sunburnt cheeks glowed with all the ardour of youthful fire; and his downy black moustache shone like silk.

" No, I have no power to thank you, noble sir," she said, her silvery voice all in a tremble. " God alone can reward you, not I, a weak woman." She dropped her eyes, her lids fell over them in beautiful, snowy semicircles, guarded by lashes long as arrows; her wondrous face bowed forward, and a delicate flush overspread it from within. Andríi knew not what to say; he wanted to say everything. He had in his mind to say it all ardently as it glowed in his heart—and could not. He felt something confining his mouth; voice and words were lacking; he felt that it was not for him, bred in the seminary and in the tumult of a roaming life, to reply fitly to such language, and was angry with his Cossack nature.

At that moment the Tatar entered the room. She had cut up the bread which the warrior had brought into small pieces on a golden plate, which she placed before her mistress. The lady glanced at her, at the bread, at her again, and then turned her eyes towards Andríi. There was a great deal in those eyes. That gentle glance, expressive of her weakness and her inability to give words to the feeling which overpowered her, was far more comprehensible to Andríi than any words. His heart suddenly grew light within him, all seemed made smooth. The mental emotions and the feelings which up to that moment he had restrained with a heavy curb, as it were, now felt themselves released, at liberty, and anxious to pour themselves out in a resistless torrent of words. Suddenly the lady turned to the Tatar, and said anxiously, " But my mother? you took her some? "

" She is asleep."

" And my father? "

" I carried him some; he said that he would come to thank the young lord in person."

She took the bread and raised it to her mouth. With inexpressible delight Andríi watched her break it with her shining fingers and eat it; but all at once he recalled the man mad with hunger, who had expired before his eyes on swallowing a morsel of bread. He turned pale and, seizing her hand, cried, " Enough! eat no more! you have not eaten for so long that too much bread will be poison to you now." And she at once dropped her hand, laid her bread upon the plate, and gazed into his eyes like a submissive child. And if any words could express—— But neither chisel, nor brush, nor mighty speech is capable of expressing what is sometimes seen in glances of maidens, nor the tender feeling which takes possession of him who receives such maiden glances.

" My queen! " exclaimed Andríi, his heart and soul filled with emotion, " what do you need? what do you wish? command me! Impose on me the most impossible task in all the world: I fly to fulfil it! Tell me to do that which it is beyond the power of man to do: I will fulfil it if I destroy myself. I will ruin myself. And I swear by the holy cross that ruin for your sake is as sweet—but no, it is impossible to say how sweet! I have three farms; half my father's droves of horses are mine; all that my mother brought my father, and which she still conceals from him—all this is mine! Not one of the Cossacks owns such weapons as I; for the pommel of my sword alone they would give their best drove of horses and three thousand sheep. And I renounce all this, I discard it, I throw it aside, I will burn and drown it, if you will but say the word, or even move your delicate black brows! But I know that I am talking madly and wide of the mark; that all this is not fitting here; that it is not for me, who have passed my life in the seminary and among the Zaporozhtzi, to speak as they speak where kings, princes, and all the best of noble knighthood have been. I can see that you are a different being from the rest of us, and far above all other boyars' wives and maiden daughters."

With growing amazement the maiden listened, losing no single word, to the frank, sincere language in which, as in a mirror, the young, strong spirit reflected itself. Each simple word of this speech, uttered in a voice which penetrated straight to the depths of her heart, was clothed in power. She advanced her beautiful face, pushed back her troublesome hair, opened her mouth, and gazed long, with parted lips. Then she tried to say something and suddenly stopped, remembering that the warrior was known by a different name; that his father, brothers, country, lay beyond, grim avengers; that the Zaporozhtzi besieging the city were terrible, and that a cruel death awaited all who were within its walls, and her eyes suddenly filled with tears. She seized a silk embroidered handkerchief and threw it over her face. In a moment it was all wet; and she sat for some time with her beautiful head thrown back, and her snowy teeth set on her lovely under-lip, as though she suddenly felt the sting of a poisonous serpent, without removing the handkerchief from her face, lest he should see her shaken with grief.

"Speak but one word to me," said Andríi, and he took her satin-skinned hand. A sparkling fire coursed through his veins at the touch, and he pressed the hand lying motionless in his.

But she still kept silence, never taking the kerchief from her face, and remaining motionless.

" Why are you so sad? Tell me, why are you so sad? "

She cast away the handkerchief, pushed aside the long hair which fell over her eyes, and poured out her heart in sad speech, in a quiet voice, like the breeze which, rising on a beautiful evening, blows through the thick growth of reeds beside the stream. They rustle, murmur, and give forth delicately mournful sounds, and the traveller, pausing in inexplicable sadness, hears them, and heeds not the fading light, nor the gay songs of the peasants which float in the air as they return from their labours in meadow and stubble-field, nor the distant rumble of the passing waggon.

" Am not I worthy of eternal pity? Is not the mother that bore me unhappy? Is it not a bitter lot which has befallen me? Art not thou a cruel executioner, fate? Thou hast brought all to my feet—the highest nobles in the land, the richest gentlemen, counts, foreign barons, all the flower of our knighthood. All loved me, and any one of them would have counted my love the greatest boon. I had but to beckon, and the best of them, the handsomest, the first in beauty and birth would have become my husband. And to none of them didst thou incline my heart, O bitter fate; but thou didst turn it against the noblest heroes of our land, and towards a stranger, towards our enemy. O most holy mother of God! for what sin dost thou so piti-lessly, mercilessly, persecute me? In abundance and superfluity of luxury my days were passed, the richest dishes and the sweetest wine were my food. And to what end was it all? What was it all for? In order that I might at last die a death more cruel than that of the meanest beggar in the kingdom? And it was not enough that I should be condemned to so horrible a fate; not enough that before my own end I should behold my father and mother perish in intolerable torment, when I would have willingly given my own life twenty times over to save them; all this was not enough, but before

my own death I must hear words of love such as I had
never before dreamed of. It was necessary that he
should break my heart with his words; that my bitter
lot should be rendered still more bitter; that my young
life should be made yet more sad; that my death should
seem even more terrible; and that, dying, I should
reproach thee still more, O cruel fate! and thee—
forgive my sin—O holy mother of God!"

As she ceased in despair, her feelings were plainly
expressed in her face. Every feature spoke of gnawing
sorrow and, from the sadly bowed brow and downcast
eyes to the tears trickling down and drying on her
softly burning cheeks, seemed to say, "There is no
happiness in this face."

"Such a thing was never heard of since the world
began. It cannot be," said Andrii, "that the best and
most beautiful of women should suffer so bitter a fate,
when she was born that all the best there is in the world
should bow before her as before a saint. No, you will
not die, you shall not die! I swear by my birth and by
all there is dear to me in the world that you shall not
die. But if it must be so; if nothing, neither strength,
nor prayer, nor heroism, will avail to avert this cruel
fate—then we will die together, and I will die first. I
will die before you, at your beauteous knees, and even in
death they shall not divide us."

"Deceive not yourself and me, noble sir," she said,
gently shaking her beautiful head; "I know, and to
my great sorrow I know but too well, that it is impossible for you to love me. I know what your duty is, and
your faith. Your father calls you, your comrades, your
country, and we are your enemies."

"And what are my father, my comrades, my country
to me?" said Andrii, with a quick movement of his
head, and straightening up his figure like a poplar
beside the river. "Be that as it may, I have no one, no
one, no one!" he repeated, with that movement of the
hand with which the Cossack expresses his determina-
tion to do some unheard-of deed, impossible to any

other man. "Who says that the Ukraine is my country? Who gave it to me for my country? Our country is the one our soul longs for, the one which is dearest of all to us. My country is—you! That is my native land, and I bear that country in my heart. I will bear it there all my life, and I will see whether any of the Cossacks can tear it thence. And I will give everything, barter everything, I will destroy myself, for that country!"

Astounded, she gazed in his eyes for a space, like a beautiful statue, and then suddenly burst out sobbing; and with the wonderful feminine impetuosity which only grand-souled, uncalculating women, created for fine impulses of the heart, are capable of, threw herself upon his neck, encircling it with her wondrous snowy arms, and wept. At that moment indistinct shouts rang through the street, accompanied by the sound of trumpets and kettledrums; but he heard them not. He was only conscious of the beauteous mouth bathing him with its warm, sweet breath, of the tears streaming down his face, and of her long, unbound perfumed hair, veiling him completely in its dark and shining silk.

At that moment the Tatar ran in with a cry of joy. "Saved, saved!" she cried, beside herself. "Our troops have entered the city. They have brought corn, millet, flour, and Zaporozhtzi in chains!" But no one heard that "our troops" had arrived in the city, or what they had brought with them, or how they had bound the Zaporozhtzi. Filled with feelings untasted as yet upon earth, Andríi kissed the sweet mouth which pressed his cheek, and the sweet mouth did not remain unresponsive. In this union of kisses they experienced that which it is given to a man to feel but once on earth.

And the Cossack was ruined. He was lost to Cossack chivalry. Never again will Zaporozhe, nor his father's house, nor the Church of God, behold him. The Ukraine will never more see the bravest of the children who have undertaken to defend her. Old Taras may tear the grey hair from his scalp-lock, and curse the day and hour in which such a son was born to dishonour him.

VII

NOISE and movement were rife in the Zaporozhian camp. At first, no one could account for the relieving army having made its way into the city; but it afterwards appeared that the Pereyaslavsky kurén, encamped before the wide gate of the town, had been dead drunk. It was no wonder that half had been killed, and the other half bound, before they knew what it was all about. Meantime the neighbouring kuréns, aroused by the tumult, succeeded in grasping their weapons; but the relieving force had already passed through the gate, and its rear ranks fired upon the sleepy and only half-sober Zaporozhtzi who were pressing in disorder upon them, and kept them back.

The Koschevoi ordered a general assembly; and when all stood in a ring and had removed their caps and become quiet, he said: " See what happened last night, brother gentles! See what drunkenness has led to! See what shame the enemy has put upon us! It is evident that, if your allowances are kindly doubled, then you are ready to stretch out at full length, and the enemies of Christ can not only take your very trousers off you, but sneeze in your faces without your hearing them! "

The Cossacks all stood with drooping heads, knowing that they were guilty; only Kukubenko, the hetman of the Nezamisky kurén, answered back. " Stop, father! " said he; " although it is not lawful to make a retort when the Koschevoi speaks before the whole army, yet it is necessary to say that that was not the state of the case. You have not been quite just in your reprimand. The Cossacks would have been guilty, and deserving of death, had they got drunk on the march, or when engaged on heavy toilsome labour during war; but we have been sitting here unoccupied, loitering in vain before the city. There was no fast or other Christian restraint; how then could it be otherwise than that a man should get drunk in idleness? There is no sin in that. But we had better show them what it is to attack innocent people. They first beat us well, and now we will beat them so that not half a dozen of them will ever see home again."

The speech of the hetman of the kurén pleased the Cossacks. They raised their drooping heads upright, and many nodded approvingly, muttering, "Kukubenko has spoken well!" And Taras Bulba, who stood not far from the Koschevoi, said: "How now, Koschevoi? Kukubenko has spoken truth. What have you to say to this?"

"What have I to say? I say, Blessed be the father of such a son! It does not need much wisdom to utter words of reproof; but much wisdom is needed to find such words as do not embitter a man's misfortune, but encourage him, restore to him his spirit, put spurs to the horse of his soul, refreshed by water. I meant myself to speak words of comfort to you, but Kukubenko has forestalled me."

"The Koschevoi has also spoken well!" rang through the ranks of the Zaporozhtzi. "His words are good," repeated others. And even the greyheads, who stood there like dark blue doves, nodded their heads and, twitching their grey moustaches, muttered softly, "That was well said."

"Listen now, gentles," continued the Koschevoi. "To take the city, by scaling its walls, or undermining them as the foreign engineers do, is not proper nor Cossack fashion. But, judging from appearances, the enemy entered the city without many provisions; they had not many waggons with them. The people in the city are hungry; they will all eat heartily, and the horses will soon devour the hay. I don't know whether their saints will fling them down anything from heaven with hayforks; God only knows that though there are a great many Catholic priests among them. By one means or another the people will seek to leave the city.

Divide yourselves, therefore, into three divisions, and take up your posts before the three gates; five kuréns before the principal gate, and three kuréns before each of the others. Let the Dadikivsky and Korsunsky kuréns go into ambush and Taras and his men into ambush too. The Titarevsky and Timoschevsky kuréns are to guard the baggage train on the right flank, the Scherbinovsky and Steblikivsky on the left, and to select from their ranks the most daring young men to face the foe. The Lyakhs are of a restless nature and cannot endure a siege, and perhaps this very day they will sally forth from the gates. Let each hetman inspect his kurén; those whose ranks are not full are to be recruited from the remains of the Pereyaslavsky kurén. Inspect them all anew. Give a loaf and a beaker to each Cossack to strengthen him. But surely every one must be satiated from last night; for all stuffed themselves so that, to tell the truth, I am only surprised that no one burst in the night. And here is one further command: if any Jew spirit-seller sells a Cossack so much as a single jug of brandy, I will nail pig's ears to his very forehead, the dog, and hang him up by his feet. To work, brothers, to work!"

Thus did the Koschevoi give his orders. All bowed to their girdles, and without putting on their caps set out for their waggons and camps. It was only when they had gone some distance that they covered themselves. All began to equip themselves: they tested their swords, poured powder from the sacks into their powder-flasks, drew up and arranged the waggons, and looked to their horses.

On his way to his band, Taras wondered what had become of Andrii; could he have been captured and bound while asleep with the others? But no, Andrii was not the man to go alive into captivity. Yet he was not to be seen among the slaughtered Cossacks. Taras pondered deeply and went past his men without hearing that some one had for some time been calling him by name. "Who wants me?" he said, finally arousing himself from his reflections. Before him stood the Jew, Yankel. " Lord colonel! lord colonel! " said the Jew in a hasty and broken voice, as though desirous of revealing something not utterly useless, " I have been in the city, lord colonel! "

Taras looked at the Jew, and wondered how he had succeeded in getting into the city. "What enemy took you there?"

" I will tell you at once," said Yankel. " As soon as I heard the uproar this morning, when the Cossacks began to fire, I seized my caftan and, without stopping to put it on, ran at the top of my speed, thrusting my arms in on the way, because I wanted to know as soon as possible the cause of the noise and why the Cossacks were firing at dawn. I ran to the very gate of the city, at the moment when the last of the army was passing through. I looked, and in command of the rearguard was Cornet Galyandóvitch. He is a man well known to me; he has owed me a hundred ducats these three years past. I ran after him, as though to claim the debt of him, and so entered the city with them."

" You entered the city, and wanted him to settle the debt! " said Bulba; " and he did not order you to be hung like a dog on the spot? "

" By heavens, he did want to hang me," replied the Jew; " his servants had already seized me and thrown a rope about my neck. But I besought the noble lord, and said that I would wait for the money as long as his lordship liked, and promised to lend him more if he would only help me to collect my debts from the other nobles; for I can tell my lord that the noble cornet had not a ducat in his pocket, although he has farms and estates and four castles and steppe-land that extends clear to Schklof; but he has not a penny, any more than a Cossack. If the Breslau Jews had not equipped him, he could never have gone on this campaign. That was the reason he did not go to the Diet."

" What did you do in the city? Did you see any of our people? "

" Certainly, there are many of them there: Itzok, Rachum, Samuel, Khaivalkh, Evrei the pawnbroker—"

" May they die, the dogs! " shouted Taras in a rage. " Why do you name your Jewish tribe to me? I ask you about our Zaporozhtzi."

" I saw none of our Zaporozhtzi; I saw only Lord Andríi."

" You saw Andríi! " shouted Bulba. " What is he doing? Where did you see him? in a dungeon? in a pit? dishonoured? bound? "

" Who would dare to bind Lord Andríi? now he is so grand a knight. I hardly recognised him. Gold on his shoulders and his belt, gold everywhere about him; as the sun shines in spring, when every bird twitters and sings in the orchard, so he shines, all gold. And his horse, which the Waiwode himself gave him, is the very best; that horse alone is worth two hundred ducats."

Bulba was petrified. " Why has he put on foreign garments? "

" He put them on because they were finer. And he rides about, and the others ride about, and he teaches them, and they teach him; like the very grandest Polish noble."

" Who forced him to this? "

" I should not say that he had been forced. Does not my lord know that he went over to them of his own free will? "

" Who went over? "

" Lord Andríi."

" Went where? "

" Went over to their side; he is now a thorough foreigner."

" You lie, you hog's ear! "

" How is it possible that I should lie? Am I a fool, that I should lie? Would I lie at the risk of my head? Do not I know that Jews are hung like dogs if they lie to nobles? "

" Then it means, according to you, he has betrayed his native land and his faith? "

" I do not say that he has betrayed anything; I merely said that he had gone over to the other side."

" You lie, you imp of a Jew! Such a deed was never known in a Christian land. You are making a mistake, dog! "

" May the grass grow upon the threshold of my house, if I am mistaken! May every one spit upon the grave of my father, my mother, my father's father, and my mother's father, if I am mistaken! If my lord wishes, I can even tell him why he went over to them."

" Why? "

" The Waiwode has a beautiful daughter. Holy Father! what a beauty! " Here the Jew tried his utmost to express beauty by extending his hands, screwing up his eyes, and twisting his mouth to one side as though tasting something on trial.

" Well, what of that? "

" He did it all for her, he went there for her sake. When a man is in love, then all things are the same to him; like the sole of a shoe which you can bend in any direction if you soak it in water."

Bulba reflected deeply. He remembered the power of weak woman—how she had ruined many a strong man, and that this was the weak point in Andríi's nature—and stood for some time in one spot, as though rooted there. " Listen, my lord, I will tell my lord all," said the Jew. " As soon as I heard the uproar, and saw them going through the city gate, I seized a string of pearls, in case of any emergency. For there are beauties and noble-women there; 'and if there are beauties and noble-women,' I said to myself, ' they will buy pearls, even if they have nothing to eat.' And, as soon as ever the cornet's servants had set me at liberty, I hastened to the Waiwode's residence to sell my pearls. I asked all manner of questions of the lady's Tatar maid; the wedding is to take place immediately, as soon as they have driven off the Zaporozhtzi. Lord Andríi has promised to drive off the Zaporovians."

"And you did not kill him on the spot, you devil's brat?" shouted Bulba.

"Why should I kill him? He went over of his own free will. What is his crime? He liked it better there, so he went there."

"And you saw him face to face?"

"Face to face, by heavens! such a magnificent warrior! more splendid than all the rest. God bless him, he knew me, and when I approached him he said at once——"

"What did he say?"

"He said—— First he beckoned me with his finger, and then he said, 'Yankel!' Lord Andríi said, 'Yankel, tell my father, tell my brother, tell all the Cossacks, all the Zaporozhtzi, everybody, that my father is no longer my father, nor my brother my brother, nor my comrades my comrades; and that I will fight them all, all.'"

"You lie, imp of a Jew!" shouted Taras, beside himself. "You lie, dog! I will kill you, Satan! Get away from here! if not, death awaits you!" So saying, Taras drew his sword.

The terrified Jew set off instantly, at the full speed of his thin, shrunken legs. He ran for a long time, without looking back, through the Cossack camp, and then far out on the deserted plain, although Taras did not chase him at all, reasoning that it was foolish to thus vent his rage on the first person who presented himself.

Then he recollected that he had seen Andríi on the previous night traversing the camp with some woman, and he bowed his grey head. Still he would not believe that so disgraceful a thing could have happened, and that his own son had betrayed his faith and soul.

Finally he placed his men in ambush in a wood—the only one which had not been burned by the Cossacks—whilst the Zaporozhians, foot and horse, set out for the three gates by three different roads. One after another the kuréns turned out: Oumansky, Popovichesky, Kanevsky, Steblikovsky, Nezamáikovsky, Gurgazif, Titarevsky, Timoschevsky. The Pereyaslavsky kurén

alone was wanting. Its Cossacks had smoked and drank
to their destruction. Some awoke to find themselves
bound in the enemy's hands; others never woke at all
but passed in their sleep into the damp earth; and the
hetman Khlib himself, minus his trousers and accoutrements, found himself in the camp of the Lyakhs.

The uproar among the Zaporozhtzi was heard in the
city. All the besieged hastened to the ramparts, and a
lively scene was presented to the Cossacks. The handsome Polish heroes thronged on the wall. The brazen
helmets of some shone like the sun, and were adorned
with feathers white as swans. Others wore pink and
blue caps, drooping over one ear, and caftans with the
sleeves thrown back, embroidered with gold. Their
weapons were richly mounted and very costly, as were
their equipments. In the front rank the Budzhakovsky
colonel stood proudly in his red cap ornamented with
gold. He was a tall, stout man, and his rich and ample
caftan hardly covered him. Near the side gate stood
another colonel. He was a dried-up little man, but his
small, piercing eyes gleamed sharply from under his
thick and shaggy brows, and as he turned quickly on
all sides, motioning boldly with his thin, withered hand,
and giving out his orders, it was evident that, in spite
of his little body, he understood military science
thoroughly. Not far from him stood a very tall cornet,
with thick moustaches and a highly-coloured com-
plexion—a noble fond of strong mead and hearty
revelry. Behind them were many nobles who had
equipped themselves, some with their own ducats,
some from the royal treasury, some with money
obtained from the Jews, by pawning everything they
found in their ancestral castles. Many too were para-
sites, whom the senators took with them to dinners for
show, and who stole silver cups from the table and the
sideboard, and when the day's display was over mounted
some noble's coach-box and drove his horses. There
were folk of all kinds there. Sometimes they had not
enough to drink, but all were equipped for war.

The Cossack ranks stood quietly before the walls. There was no gold about them, save where it shone on the hilt of a sword or the mountings of a gun. The Zaporozhtzi were not given to decking themselves out gaily for battle: their coats-of-mail and garments were plain, and their black-bordered red-crowned caps showed darkly in the distance.

Two men—Okhrim Nasch and Mikiga Golokopui-tenko—advanced from the Zaporozhian ranks. One was quite young, the other older; both fierce in words, and not bad specimens of Cossacks in action. They were followed by Demid Popovitch, a strongly built Cossack who had been hanging about the Setch for a long time, after having been in Adrianople and undergoing a great deal in the course of his life. He had been burned, and had escaped to the Setch with blackened head and singed moustaches. But Popovitch recovered, let his hair grow, raised moustaches thick and black as pitch, and was a stout fellow, according to his own biting speech.

" Red jackets on all the army, but I should like to know what sort of men are under them," he cried.

" I will show you," shouted the stout colonel from above. " I will capture the whole of you. Surrender your guns and horses, slaves. Did you see how I caught your men?—Bring out a Zaporozhetz on the wall for them to see."

And they led out a Zaporozhetz bound with stout cords.

Before them stood Khlib, the hetman of the Pereya-slavsky kurén, without his trousers or accoutrements, just as they had captured him in his drunken sleep. He bowed his head in shame before the Cossacks at his nakedness, and at having been thus taken like a dog, while asleep. His hair had turned grey in one night.

" Grieve not, Khlib: we will rescue you," shouted the Cossacks from below.

" Grieve not, friend," cried the hetman Borodaty. " It is not your fault that they caught you naked: that misfortune might happen to any man. But it is a disgrace to them that they should have exposed you to dishonour, and not covered your nakedness decently."

" You seem to be a brave army when you have people who are asleep to fight," remarked Golokopuitenko, glancing at the ramparts.

" Wait a bit, we'll singe your top-knots for you! " was the reply.

" I should like to see them singe our scalp locks! " said Popovitch, prancing about before them on his horse; and then, glancing at his comrades, he added, " Well, perhaps the Lyakhs speak the truth: if that fat-bellied fellow there leads them, they will all find a good shelter."

" Why do you think they will find a good shelter? " asked the Cossacks, knowing that Popovitch was probably preparing some repartee.

" Because the whole army will hide behind him; and the devil himself couldn't help you to reach any one with your spear through that belly of his! "

The Cossacks laughed, some of them shaking their heads and saying, " What a fellow Popovitch is for a joke! but now—— " But the Cossacks had not time to explain what they meant by that " now."

" Fall back, fall back quickly from the wall! " shouted the Koschevoi, seeing that the Lyakhs could not endure these biting words, and that the colonel was waving his hand.

The Cossacks had hardly retreated from the wall before the grape-shot rained down. On the ramparts all was excitement, and the grey-haired Waiwode himself appeared on horseback. The gates opened and the garrison sallied forth. In the van came hussars in orderly ranks, behind them the horsemen in armour, and then the heroes in brazen helmets; after whom rode singly the highest nobility, each man accoutred as he pleased. These haughty nobles would not mingle in the ranks with others, and such of them as had no commands rode apart with their own immediate following.

Next came more companies, and after these the cornet,
then more files of men, and the stout colonel; and in
the rear of the whole force the little colonel.

"Keep them from forming in line!" shouted the
Koschevoi; "let all the kuréns attack them at once!
Block the other gate! Titarevsky kurén, fall on one
flank! Dyadovsky kurén, charge on the other! Attack
them in the rear, Kukubenko and Palivod! Check them,
break them!" The Cossacks attacked on all sides,
throwing the Lyakhs into confusion and getting confused themselves. They did not even give the foe time
to fire; it came to swords and spears at once. All fought
hand to hand, and each man had an opportunity to
distinguish himself.

Demid Popovitch speared three soldiers, and struck
two of the highest nobles from their saddles, saying,
"Good horses! I have long wanted just such horses."
And he drove the horses far afield, shouting to the
Cossacks standing about to catch them. Then he
rushed again into the fray, fell upon the dismounted
nobles, slew one, and throwing his lasso round the neck
of the other, tied him to his saddle and dragged him
over the plain, after having taken from him his sword
with its rich hilt and removed from his girdle a whole
bag of ducats.

Kobita, a good Cossack, though still very young,
attacked one of the bravest men in the Polish army,
and they fought long together. They grappled, and the
Cossack mastering his foe, and throwing him down,
stabbed him in the breast with his sharp Turkish knife.
But he did not look out for himself, and a bullet struck
him on the temple. The man who struck him down was
the most distinguished of the nobles, the handsomest
scion of an ancient and princely race. Like a stately
poplar, he bestrode his dun-coloured steed, and many
heroic deeds did he perform. He cut two Cossacks in
twain. Fedor Korzh, the brave Cossack, he overthrew
together with his horse, shooting the steed and picking
off the rider with his spear. Many heads and hands did

he hew off; and slew Kobita by sending a bullet through his temple.

"There's a man I should like to measure strength with!" shouted Kukubenko, the hetman of the Nezamáikovsky kurén. Spurring his horse, he dashed straight at the Pole's back, shouting loudly, so that all who stood near shuddered at that unearthly yell. The boyard tried to wheel his horse suddenly and face him, but the horse would not obey him; scared by the terrible cry, it bounded aside, and the Lyakh received Kukubenko's fire. The ball struck him in the shoulder-blade, and he rolled from his saddle. Even then he did not surrender and strove to deal his enemy a blow, but his hand was weak. Kukubenko, taking his heavy sword in both hands, thrust it through his mouth. The sword, breaking out two teeth, cut the tongue in twain, pierced the windpipe, and penetrated deep into the earth, nailing him to the ground. His noble blood, red as viburnum berries beside the river, welled forth in a stream staining his yellow, gold-embroidered caftan. But Kukubenko had already left him, and was forcing his way, with his Nezamáikovsky kurén, towards another group.

"He has left untouched rich plunder," said Borodaty, hetman of the Oumansky kurén, leaving his men and going to the place where the nobleman killed by Kukubenko lay. "I have killed seven nobles with my own hand, but such spoil I never beheld on any one." Prompted by greed, Borodaty bent down to strip off the rich armour, and had already secured the Turkish knife set with precious stones, and taken from the foe's belt a purse of ducats, and from his breast a silver case containing a maiden's curl, cherished tenderly as a love-token. But he heeded not how the red-faced cornet, whom he had already once hurled from the saddle and given a good blow as a remembrance, flew upon him from behind. The cornet swung his arm with all his might, and brought his sword down upon Borodaty's bent neck. Greed led to no good: the head rolled off, and the body fell headless, sprinkling the earth with blood far and wide; whilst the Cossack soul ascended, indignant and surprised at having so soon quitted so stout a frame. The cornet had not succeeded in seizing the hetman's head by its scalp-lock, and fastening it to his saddle, before an avenger had arrived.

As a hawk floating in the sky, sweeping in great circles with his mighty wings, suddenly remains poised in air, in one spot, and thence darts down like an arrow upon the shrieking quail, so Taras's son Ostap darted suddenly upon the cornet and flung a rope about his neck with one cast. The cornet's red face became a still deeper purple as the cruel noose compressed his throat, and he tried to use his pistol; but his convulsively quivering hand could not aim straight, and the bullet flew wild across the plain. Ostap immediately unfastened a silken cord which the cornet carried at his saddle bow to bind prisoners, and having with it bound him hand and foot, attached the cord to his saddle and dragged him across the field, calling on all the Cossacks of the Oumansky kurén to come and render the last honours to their hetman.

When the Oumantzi heard that the hetman of their kurén, Borodaty, was no longer among the living, they deserted the field of battle, rushed to secure his body, and consulted at once as to whom they should select as their leader. At length they said, " But why consult? It is impossible to find a better leader than Bulba's son, Ostap; he is younger than all the rest of us, it is true; but his judgment is equal to that of the eldest."

Ostap, taking off his cap, thanked his comrades for the honour, and did not decline it on the ground of youth or inexperience, knowing that war time is no fitting season for that; but instantly ordered them straight to the fray, and soon showed them that not in vain had they chosen him as hetman. The Lyakhs felt that the matter was growing too hot for them, and retreated across the plain in order to form again at its other end. But the little colonel signalled to the reserve of four hundred, stationed at the gate, and these rained shot upon the Cossacks. To little purpose, however, their shot only taking effect on the Cossack oxen, which were gazing wildly upon the battle. The frightened oxen, bellowing with fear, dashed into the camp, breaking the line of waggons and trampling on many. But Taras, emerging from ambush at the moment with his troops, headed off the infuriated cattle, which, startled by his yell, swooped down upon the Polish troops, overthrew the cavalry, and crushed and dispersed them all.

"Thank you, oxen!" cried the Zaporozhtzi; "you served us on the march, and now you serve us in war." And they attacked the foe with fresh vigour killing many of the enemy. Several distinguished themselves —Metelitza and Schilo, both of the Pisarenki, Vovtuzenko, and many others. The Lyakhs seeing that matters were going badly for them flung away their banners and shouted for the city gates to be opened. With a screeching sound the iron-bound gates swung open and received the weary and dust-covered riders, flocking like sheep into a fold. Many of the Zaporozhtzi would have pursued them, but Ostap stopped his Oumantzi, saying, "Farther, farther from the walls, brother gentles! it is not well to approach them too closely." He spoke truly; for from the ramparts the foe rained and poured down everything which came to hand, and many were struck. At that moment the Koschevoi came up and congratulated him, saying, "Here is the new hetman leading the army like an old one!" Old Bulba glanced round to see the new hetman, and beheld Ostap sitting on his horse at the head of the Oumantzi, his cap on one side and the hetman's staff in his hand. "Who ever saw the like!" he exclaimed; and the old man rejoiced, and began to thank all the Oumantzi for the honour they had conferred upon his son.

The Cossacks retired, preparing to go into camp; but the Lyakhs showed themselves again on the city ramparts with tattered mantles. Many rich caftans were spotted with blood, and dust covered the brazen helmets.

" Have you bound us? " cried the Zaporozhtzi to them from below.

" We will do so! " shouted the big colonel from above, showing them a rope. The weary, dust-covered warriors ceased not to threaten, nor the most zealous on both sides to exchange fierce remarks.

At length all dispersed. Some, weary with battle, stretched themselves out to rest; others sprinkled their wounds with earth, and bound them with kerchiefs and rich stuffs captured from the enemy. Others, who were fresher, began to inspect the corpses and to pay them the last honours. They dug graves with swords and spears, brought earth in their caps and the skirts of their garments, laid the Cossacks' bodies out decently, and covered them up in order that the ravens and eagles might not claw out their eyes. But binding the bodies of the Lyakhs, as they came to hand, to the tails of horses, they let these loose on the plain, pursuing them and beating them for some time. The infuriated horses flew over hill and hollow, through ditch and brook, dragging the bodies of the Poles, all covered with blood and dust, along the ground.

All the kuréns sat down in circles in the evening, and talked for a long time of their deeds, and of the achievements which had fallen to the share of each, for repetition by strangers and posterity. It was long before they lay down to sleep; and longer still before old Taras, meditating what it might signify that Andrii was not among the foe, lay down. Had the Judas been ashamed to come forth against his own countrymen? or had the Jew been deceiving him, and had he simply gone into the city against his will? But then he recollected that there were no bounds to woman's influence upon Andrii's heart; he felt ashamed, and swore a mighty oath to himself against the fair Pole who had bewitched his son. And he would have kept his oath. He would not have looked at her beauty; he would have dragged her forth by her thick and splendid hair; he would have trailed her after him over all the plain, among all the Cossacks.

Her beautiful shoulders and bosom, white as fresh-fallen snow upon the mountain-tops, would have been crushed to earth and covered with blood and dust. Her lovely body would have been torn to pieces. But Taras, who did not foresee what God prepares for man on the morrow, began to grow drowsy, and finally fell asleep. The Cossacks still talked among themselves; and the sober sentinel stood all night long beside the fire without blinking and keeping a good look out on all sides.

VIII

THE sun had not ascended midway in the heavens when all the army assembled in a group. News had come from the Setch that during the Cossacks' absence the Tatars had plundered it completely, unearthed the treasures which were kept concealed in the ground, killed or carried into captivity all who had remained behind, and straightway set out, with all the flocks and droves of horses they had collected, for Perekop. One Cossack only, Maksin Galodukha, had broken loose from the Tatars' hands, stabbed the Mirza, seized his bag of sequins, and on a Tatar horse, in Tatar garments, had fled from his pursuers for two nights and a day and a half, ridden his horse to death, obtained another, killed that one too, and arrived at the Zaporozhian camp upon a third, having learned upon the road that the Zaporozhtzi were before Dubno. He could only manage to tell them that this misfortune had taken place; but as to how it happened—whether the remaining Zaporozhtzi had been carousing after Cossack fashion, and had been carried drunk into captivity, and how the Tatars were aware of the spot where the treasures of the army were concealed—he was too exhausted to say. Extremely fatigued, his body swollen, and his face scorched and weatherbeaten, he had fallen down, and a deep sleep had overpowered him.

In such cases it was customary for the Cossacks
to pursue the robbers at once, endeavouring to overtake them on the road; for, let the prisoners once be
got to the bazaars of Asia Minor, Smyrna, or the island
of Crete, and God knows in what places the tufted heads
of Zaporozhtzi might not be seen. This was the occasion of the Cossacks' assembling. They all stood to a
man with their caps on; for they had not met to listen
to the commands of their hetman, but to take counsel
together as equals among equals. " Let the old men
first advise," was shouted in the crowd. " Let the
Koschevoi give his opinion," cried others.

The Koschevoi, taking off his cap and speaking not
as commander, but as a comrade among comrades,
thanked all the Cossacks for the honour, and said,
" There are among us many experienced men and much
wisdom; but since you have thought me worthy, my
counsel is not to lose time in pursuing the Tatars, for
you know yourselves what the Tatar is. He will not
pause with his stolen booty to await our coming, but
will vanish in a twinkling, so that you can find no trace
of him. Therefore my advice is to go. We have had
good sport here. The Lyakhs now know what Cossacks
are. We have avenged our faith to the extent of our
ability; there is not much to satisfy greed in the
famished city, and so my advice is to go."

" To go," rang heavily through the Zaporozhian
kuréns. But such words did not suit Taras Bulba at all;
and he brought his frowning, iron-grey brows still lower
down over his eyes, brows like bushes growing on dark
mountain heights, whose crowns are suddenly covered
with sharp northern frost.

" No, Koschevoi, your counsel is not good," said he.
" You cannot say that. You have evidently forgotten
that those of our men captured by the Lyakhs will
remain prisoners. You evidently wish that we should
not heed the first holy law of comradeship; that we
should leave our brethren to be flayed alive, or carried
about through the towns and villages after their Cossack

bodies have been quartered, as was done with the hetman and the bravest Russian warriors in the Ukraine. Have the enemy not desecrated the holy things sufficiently without that? What are we? I ask you all, what sort of a Cossack is he who would desert his comrade in misfortune, and let him perish like a dog in a foreign land? If it has come to such a pass that no one has any confidence in Cossack honour, permitting men to spit upon his grey moustache, and upbraid him with offensive words, then let no one blame me; I will remain here alone."

All the Zaporozhtzi who stood there wavered.

" And have you forgotten, brave comrades," said the Koschevoi, " that the Tatars also have comrades of ours in their hands; that if we do not rescue them now their lives will be sacrificed in eternal imprisonment among the infidels, which is worse than the most cruel death? Have you forgotten that they now hold all our treasure, won by Christian blood? "

The Cossacks reflected, not knowing what to say. None of them wished to deserve ill repute. Then there stepped out in front of them the oldest in years of all the Zaporozhian army, Kasyan Bovdug. He was respected by all the Cossacks. Twice had he been chosen Koschevoi, and had also been a stout warrior; but he had long been old, and had ceased to go upon raids. Neither did the old man like to give advice to any one; but loved to lie upon his side in the circle of Cossacks, listening to tales of every occurrence on the Cossack marches. He never joined in the conversation, but only listened, and pressed the ashes with his finger in his short pipe, which never left his mouth; and would sit so long with his eyes half open, that the Cossacks never knew whether he were asleep or still listening. He always stayed at home during their raids, but this time the old man had joined the army. He had waved his hand in Cossack fashion, and said, " Wherever you go, I am going too; perhaps I may be of some service to the Cossack nation." All the Cossacks became silent when he now stepped forward before the assembly, for it was long since any speech from him had been heard. Every one wanted to know what Bovdug had to say.

" It is my turn to speak a word, brother gentles," he began: " listen, my children, to an old man. The Koschevoi spoke well as the head of the Cossack army; being bound to protect it, and in respect to the treasures of the army he could say nothing wiser. That is so! Let that be my first remark; but now listen to my second. And this is my second remark: Taras spoke even more truly. God grant him many years, and that such leaders may be plentiful in the Ukraine! A Cossack's first duty and first honour is to guard comradeship. Never in all my life, brother gentles, have I heard of any Cossack deserting or betraying any of his comrades. Both those made captive at the Setch and these taken here are our comrades. Whether they be few or many, it makes no difference; all are our comrades, and all are dear to us. So this is my speech: Let those to whom the prisoners captured by the Tatars are dear set out after the Tatars; and let those to whom the captives of the Poles are dear, and who do not care to desert a righteous cause, stay behind. The Koschevoi, in accordance with his duty, will accompany one half in pursuit of the Tatars, and the other half can choose a hetman to lead them. But if you will heed the words of an old man, there is no man fitter to be the commanding hetman than Taras Bulba. Not one of us is his equal in heroism."

Thus spoke Bovdug, and paused; and all the Cossacks rejoiced that the old man had in this manner brought them to an agreement. All flung up their caps and shouted, " Thanks, father! He kept silence for a long, long time, but he has spoken at last. Not in vain did he say, when we prepared for this expedition, that he might be useful to the Cossack nation: even so it has come to pass! "

" Well, are you agreed upon anything? " asked the Koschevoi.

" We are all agreed! " cried the Cossacks.

" Then the council is at an end? "

" At an end! " cried the Cossacks.

" Then listen to the military command, children," said the Koschevoi, stepping forward, and putting on his cap; whilst all the Cossacks took off theirs, and stood with uncovered heads, and with eyes fixed upon the earth, as was always the custom among them when the leader prepared to speak. " Now divide yourselves, brother gentles! Let those who wish to go stand on the right, and those who wish to stay, on the left. Where the majority of a kurén goes there its officers are to go: if the minority of a kurén goes over, it must be added to another kurén."

Then they began to take up their positions, some to the right and some to the left. Whither the majority of a kurén went thither the hetman went also; and the minority attached itself to another kurén. It came out pretty even on both sides. Those who wished to remain were nearly the whole of the Nezamáikovsky kurén, the entire Oumansky kurén, the entire Kanevsky kurén, and the larger half of the Popóvitchvsky, the Timoschevsky and the Steblikivsky kuréns. All the rest preferred to go in pursuit of the Tatars. On both sides there were many stout and brave Cossacks. Among those who decided to follow the Tatars were Tcherevaty, and those good old Cossacks Pokotípole, Lemísch, and Prokopovitch Koma. Demid Popovitch also went with that party, because he could not sit long in one place: he had tried his hand on the Lyakhs and wanted to try it on the Tatars also. The hetman of kuréns were Nostiugán, Pókruischka, Nevnimsky, and numerous brave and renowned Cossacks who wished to test their swords and muscles in an encounter with the Tatars. There were likewise many brave Cossacks among those who preferred to remain, including the kurén hetmans, Demitrovitch, Kukubenko, Vertíkhvist, Balán, and Ostap Bulba. Besides these there were plenty of stout and distinguished warriors: Vovtuzenko, Tcherevitchénko, Stepan Guska, Okhrim Guska, Vikola Gonstiy, Zadorozhniy, Metélitza, Ivan Zakrutíguba, Mosiy Schilo, Degtyarénko, Sidorenko, Pisarenko, a second Pisarenko, and still another Pisarenko, and many others. They were all great travellers; they had visited the shores of Anatolia, the salt marshes and steppes of the Crimea, all the rivers great and small which empty into the Dnieper, and all the fords and islands of the Dnieper; they had been in Moldavia, Wallachia, and Turkey; they had sailed all over the Black Sea, in their double-ruddered Cossack boats; they had attacked with fifty skiffs in line the tallest and richest ships; they had sunk many a Turkish galley, and had burnt much, very much powder in their day; more than once they had made foot-bandages from velvets and rich stuffs; more than once they had beaten buckles for their girdles out of sequins. Every one of them had drunk and revelled away what would have sufficed any other for a whole lifetime, and had nothing to show for it. They spent it all, like Cossacks, in treating all the world, and in hiring music that every one might be merry. Even now few of them had amassed any property: some caskets, cups, and bracelets were hidden beneath the reeds on the islands of the Dnieper in order that the Tatars might not find them if by mishap they should succeed in falling suddenly on the Setch; but it would have been difficult for the Tatar to find them, for the owners themselves had forgotten where they had buried them. Such were the Cossacks who wished to remain and take vengeance on the Lyakhs for their trusty comrades and the faith of Christ. The old Cossack Bovdug wished also to remain with them, saying, " I am not of an age to pursue the Tatars, but this is a place to meet a good Cossack death. I have long prayed God that when my life was to end I might end it in battle for a holy and Christian cause. And so it has come to pass. There can be no more glorious end in any other place for the aged Cossack."

When they had all separated, and were ranged in

two lines on opposite sides, the Koschevoi passed through the ranks, and said, " Well, brother gentles, are the two parties satisfied with each other? "

" All satisfied, father! " replied the Cossacks.

" Then kiss each other, and bid each other farewell; for God knows whether you will ever see each other alive again. Obey your hetman, but you know yourselves what you have to do: you know yourselves what Cossack honour requires."

And all the Cossacks kissed each other. The hetmans first began it. Stroking down their grey moustaches, they kissed each other, making the sign of the cross, and then, grasping hands firmly, wanted to ask of each other, " Well, brother, shall we see one another again or not? " But they did not ask the question: they kept silence, and both grey-heads were lost in thought. Then the Cossacks took leave of each other to the last man, knowing that there was a great deal of work before them all. Yet they were not obliged to part at once: they would have to wait until night in order not to let the Lyakhs perceive the diminution in the Cossack army. Then all went off, by kuréns, to dine.

After dinner, all who had the prospect of the journey before them lay down to rest, and fell into a deep and long sleep, as though foreseeing that it was the last sleep they should enjoy in such security. They slept even until sunset; and when the sun had gone down and it had grown somewhat dusky, began to tar the waggons. All being in readiness, they sent the waggons ahead, and having pulled off their caps once more to their comrades, quietly followed the baggage train. The cavalry, without shouts or whistles to the horses, tramped lightly after the foot-soldiers, and all soon vanished in the darkness. The only sound was the dull thud of horses' hoofs, or the squeak of some wheel which had not got into working order, or had not been properly tarred amid the darkness.

Their comrades stood for some time waving their hands, though nothing was visible. But when they returned to their camping places and saw by the light of the gleaming stars that half the waggons were gone, and many of their comrades, each man's heart grew sad; all became involuntarily pensive, and drooped their heads towards the earth.

Taras saw how troubled were the Cossack ranks, and that sadness, unsuited to brave men, had begun to quietly master the Cossack hearts; but he remained silent. He wished to give them time to become accustomed to the melancholy caused by their parting from their comrades; but, meanwhile, he was preparing to rouse them at one blow, by a loud battle-cry in Cossack fashion, in order that good cheer might return to the soul of each with greater strength than before. Of this only the Slav nature, a broad, powerful nature, which is to others what the sea is to small rivulets, is capable. In stormy times it roars and thunders, raging, and raising such waves as weak rivers cannot throw up; but when it is windless and quiet, it spreads its boundless glassy surface, clearer than any river, a constant delight to the eye.

Taras ordered his servants to unload one of the waggons which stood apart. It was larger and stronger than any other in the Cossack camp; two stout tires encircled its mighty wheels. It was heavily laden, covered with horsecloths and strong wolf-skins, and firmly bound with tightly drawn tarred ropes. In the waggon were flasks and casks of good old wine, which had long lain in Taras's cellar. He had brought it along, in case a moment should arrive when some deed awaited them worthy of being handed down to posterity, so that each Cossack, to the very last man, might quaff it, and be inspired with sentiments befitting the occasion. On receiving his command, the servants hastened to the waggon, hewed asunder the stout ropes with their swords, removed the thick wolf-skins and horsecloths, and drew forth the flasks and casks.

" Take them all," said Bulba, " all there are; take them, that every one may be supplied. Take jugs, or the pails for watering the horses; take sleeve or cap;

but if you have nothing else, then hold your two hands under."

All the Cossacks seized something: one took a jug, another a pail, another a sleeve, another a cap, and another held both hands. Taras's servants, making their way among the ranks, poured out for all from the casks and flasks. But Taras ordered them not to drink until he should give the signal for all to drink together. It was evident that he wished to say something. He knew that however good in itself the old wine might be and however fitted to strengthen the spirit of man, yet, if a suitable speech were linked with it, then the strength of the wine and of the spirit would be doubled.

"I treat you, brother gentles," thus spoke Bulba, "not in honour of your having made me hetman, however great such an honour may be, nor in honour of our parting from our comrades. To do both would be fitting at a fitting time; but the moment before us is not such a time. The work before us is great both in labour and in glory for the Cossacks. Therefore let us drink all together, let us drink before all else to the holy orthodox faith, that the day may finally come when it may be spread over all the world, and that everywhere there may be but one faith, and that all Mussulmans may become Christians. And let us also drink together to the Setch, that it may stand long for the ruin of the Mussulmans, and that every year there may issue forth from it young men, each better, each handsomer than the other. And let us drink to our own glory, that our grandsons and their sons may say that there were once men who were not ashamed of comradeship, and who never betrayed each other. Now to the faith, brother gentles, to the faith!"

"To the faith!" cried those standing in the ranks hard by, with thick voices. "To the faith!" those more distant took up the cry; and all, both young and old, drank to the faith.

"To the Setch!" said Taras, raising his hand high above his head.

" To the Setch! " echoed the foremost ranks. " To the Setch! " said the old men, softly, twitching their grey moustaches; and eagerly as young hawks, the youths repeated, " To the Setch! " And the distant plain heard how the Cossacks mentioned their Setch.

" Now a last draught, comrades, to the glory of all Christians now living in the world! "

And every Cossack drank a last draught to the glory of all Christians in the world. And among all the ranks in all the kuréns they long repeated, " To all the Christians in the world! "

The pails were empty, but the Cossacks still stood with their hands uplifted. Although the eyes of all gleamed brightly with the wine, they were thinking deeply. Not of greed or the spoils of war were they thinking now, nor of who would be lucky enough to get ducats, fine weapons, embroidered caftans, and Tcherkessian horses; but they meditated like eagles perched upon the rocky crests of mountains, from which the distant sea is visible, dotted, as with tiny birds, with galleys, ships, and every sort of vessel, bounded only by the scarcely visible lines of shore, with their ports like gnats and their forests like fine grass. Like eagles they gazed out on all the plain, with their fate darkling in the distance. All the plain, with its slopes and roads, will be covered with their white projecting bones, lavishly washed with their Cossack blood, and strewn with shattered waggons and with broken swords and spears; the eagles will swoop down and tear out their Cossack eyes. But there is one grand advantage: not a single noble deed will be lost, and the Cossack glory will not vanish like the tiniest grain of powder from a gun-barrel. The guitar-player with grey beard falling upon his breast, and perhaps a white-headed old man still full of ripe, manly strength will come, and will speak his low, strong words of them. And their glory will resound through all the world, and all who are born thereafter will speak of them; for the word of power is carried afar, ringing like a booming brazen bell, in which the maker has mingled much rich, pure silver, that its beautiful sound may be borne far and wide through the cities, villages, huts, and palaces, summoning all betimes to holy prayer.

IX

IN the city, no one knew that one-half of the Cossacks had gone in pursuit of the Tatars. From the tower of the town hall the sentinel only perceived that a part of the waggons had been dragged into the forest; but it was thought that the Cossacks were preparing an ambush—a view taken by the French engineer also. Meanwhile, the Koschevoi's words proved not unfounded, for a scarcity of provisions arose in the city. According to a custom of past centuries, the army did not separate as much as was necessary. They tried to make a sortie; but half of those who did so were instantly killed by the Cossacks, and the other half driven back into the city with no results. But the Jews availed themselves of the opportunity to find out everything; whither and why the Zaporozhtzi had departed, and with what leaders, and which particular kuréns, and their number, and how many had remained on the spot, and what they intended to do; in short, within a few minutes all was known in the city.

The besieged took courage, and prepared to offer battle. Taras had already divined it from the noise and movement in the city, and hastened about, making his arrangements, forming his men, and giving orders and instructions. He ranged the kuréns in three camps, surrounding them with the waggons as bulwarks—a formation in which the Zaporozhtzi were invincible—ordered two kuréns into ambush, and drove sharp stakes, broken guns, and fragments of spears into a part of the plain, with a view to forcing the enemy's cavalry upon it if an opportunity should present itself. When all was done which was necessary, he made a speech to the Cossacks, not for the purpose of encouraging and freshening up their spirits—he knew their souls were strong without that—but simply because he wished to tell them all he had upon his heart.

" I want to tell you, brother gentles, what our brotherhood is. You have heard from your fathers and grandfathers in what honour our land has always been held by all. We made ourselves known to the Greeks, and we took gold from Constantinople, and our cities were luxurious, and we had, too, our temples, and our princes—the princes of the Russian people, our own princes, not Catholic unbelievers. But the Mussulmans took all; all vanished, and we remained defenceless; yea, like a widow after the death of a powerful husband: defenceless was our land as well as ourselves! Such was the time, comrades, when we joined hands in a brotherhood: that is what our fellowship consists in. There is no more sacred brotherhood. The father loves his children, the mother loves her children, the children love their father and mother; but this is not like that, brothers. The wild beast also loves its young. But a man can be related only by similarity of mind and not of blood. There have been brotherhoods in other lands, but never any such brotherhoods as on our Russian soil. It has happened to many of you to be in foreign lands. You look: there are people there also, God's creatures, too; and you talk with them as with the men of your own country. But when it comes to saying a hearty word—you will see. No! they are sensible people, but not the same; the same kind of people, and yet not the same! No, brothers, to love as the Russian soul loves, is to love not with the mind or anything else, but with all that God has given, all that is within you. Ah! " said Taras, and waved his hand, and wiped his grey head, and twitched his moustache, and then went on: " No, no one else can love in that way! I know that baseness has now made its way into our land. Men care only to have their ricks of grain and hay, and their droves of horses, and that their mead may be safe in their cellars; they adopt, the devil only knows what Mussulman customs. They speak scornfully with their tongues. They care not to speak their real thoughts with their own countrymen. They sell their own things to their own comrades, like soulless creatures in the market-place. The favour of a foreign king, and not even of a king, but the poor favour of a Polish magnate, who beats them on the mouth with his yellow shoe, is dearer to them than all brotherhood. But the very meanest of these vile men, whoever he may be, given over though he be to vileness and slavishness, even he, brothers, has some grains of Russian feeling; and they will assert themselves some day. And then the wretched man will beat his breast with his hands; and will tear his hair, cursing his vile life loudly, and ready to expiate his disgraceful deeds with torture. Let them know what brotherhood means on Russian soil! And if it has come to the point that a man must die for his brotherhood, it is not fit that any of them should die so. No! none of them. It is not a fit thing for their mouse-like natures."

Thus spoke the hetman; and after he had finished his speech he still continued to shake his head, which had grown grey in Cossack service. All who stood there were deeply affected by this speech, which went to their very hearts. The oldest in the ranks stood motionless, their grey heads drooping. Tears trickled quietly from their aged eyes; they wiped them slowly away with their sleeves, and then all, as if with one consent, waved their hands in the air at the same moment, and shook their experienced heads. For it was evident that old Taras recalled to them many of the best-known and finest traits of the heart in a man who has become wise through suffering, toil, daring, and every earthly misfortune, or, though unknown to them, of many things felt by young, pure spirits, to the eternal joy of the parents who bore them.

But the army of the enemy was already marching out

of the city, sounding drums and trumpets; and the nobles, with their arms akimbo, were riding forth too, surrounded by innumerable servants. The stout colonel gave his orders, and they began to advance briskly on the Cossack camps, pointing their matchlocks threateningly. Their eyes flashed, and they were brilliant with brass armour. As soon as the Cossacks saw that they had come within gunshot, their matchlocks thundered all together, and they continued to fire without cessation.

The detonations resounded through the distant fields and meadows, merging into one continuous roar. The whole plain was shrouded in smoke, but the Zaporozhtzi continued to fire without drawing breath—the rear ranks doing nothing but loading the guns and handing them to those in front, thus creating amazement among the enemy, who could not understand how the Cossacks fired without reloading. Amid the dense smoke which enveloped both armies, it could not be seen how first one and then another dropped: but the Lyakhs felt that the balls flew thickly, and that the affair was growing hot; and when they retreated to escape from the smoke and see how matters stood, many were missing from their ranks, but only two or three out of a hundred were killed on the Cossack side. Still the Cossacks went on firing off their matchlocks without a moment's intermission. Even the foreign engineers were amazed at tactics heretofore unknown to them, and said then and there, in the presence of all, " These Zaporozhtzi are brave fellows. That is the way men in other lands ought to fight." And they advised that the cannon should at once be turned on the camps. Heavily roared the iron cannon with their wide throats; the earth hummed and trembled far and wide, and the smoke lay twice as heavy over the plain. They smelt the reek of the powder among the squares and streets in the most distant as well as the nearest quarters of the city. But those who laid the cannon pointed them too high, and the shot describing too wide a curve flew over the heads of the camps, and buried themselves deep in the earth at a distance, tearing the ground, and throwing the black soil high in the air. At the sight of such lack of skill the French engineer tore his hair, and undertook to lay the cannon himself, heeding not the Cossack bullets which showered round him.

Taras saw from afar that destruction menaced the whole Nezamáikovsky and Steblikivsky kuréns, and gave a ringing shout, " Get away from the waggons instantly, and mount your horses! " But the Cossacks would not have succeeded in effecting both these movements if Ostap had not dashed into the midst of the foe and wrenched the linstocks from six cannoneers. But he could not wrench them from the other four, for the Lyakhs drove him back. Meanwhile the foreign captain had taken the match in his own hand to fire off the largest cannon, such a cannon as none of the Cossacks had ever beheld before. It looked horrible with its wide mouth, and a thousand deaths poured forth from it. And as it thundered, the three others followed, shaking in fourfold earthquake the dully responsive earth. Much woe did they cause. For more than one Cossack wailed the aged mother, beating with bony hands her feeble breast; more than one widow was left in Glukhof, Nemirof, Chernigof, and other cities. The loving woman will hasten forth every day to the bazaar, grasping at all passers-by, scanning the face of each to see if there be not among them one dearer than all; but though many an army will pass through the city, never among them will a single one of all their dearest be.

Half the Nezamáikovsky kurén was as if it had never been. As the hail suddenly beats down a field where every ear of grain shines like purest gold, so were they beaten down.

How the Cossacks hastened thither! How they all started up! How raged Kukubenko, the hetman, when he saw that the best half of his kurén was no more! He fought his way with his remaining Nezamáikovtzi

to the very midst of the fray, cut down in his wrath, like
a cabbage, the first man he met, hurled many a rider
from his steed, piercing both horse and man with his
lance; and making his way to the gunners, captured
one of the cannons. Here he found the hetman of the
Oumansky kurén, and Stepan Guska, hard at work,
having already seized the largest cannon. He left those
Cossacks there, and plunged with his own into another
mass of the foe, making a lane through it. Where the
Nezamáikovtzi passed there was a street; where they
turned about there was a square as where streets
meet. The foemen's ranks were visibly thinning, and
the Lyakhs falling in sheaves. Beside the waggons
stood Vovtuzenko, and in front Tcherevitchenko, and
by the more distant ones Degtyarenko; and behind
them the kurén hetman, Vertikhvist. Degtyarenko had
pierced two Lyakhs with his spear, and now attacked
a third, a stout antagonist. Agile and strong was the
Lyakh, with glittering arms, and accompanied by fifty
followers. He fell fiercely upon Degtyarenko, struck
him to the earth, and, flourishing his sword above him,
cried, "There is not one of you Cossack dogs who has
dared to oppose me."

"Here is one," said Mosiy Schilo, and stepped forward. He was a muscular Cossack, who had often
commanded at sea, and undergone many vicissitudes.
The Turks had once seized him and his men at Trebi-
zond, and borne them captives to the galleys, where
they bound them hand and foot with iron chains, gave
them no food for a week at a time, and made them
drink sea-water. The poor prisoners endured and
suffered all, but would not renounce their orthodox
faith. Their hetman, Mosiy Schilo, could not bear it:
he trampled the Holy Scriptures under foot, wound the
vile turban about his sinful head, and became the
favourite of a pasha, steward of a ship, and ruler over
all the galley slaves. The poor slaves sorrowed greatly
thereat, for they knew that if he had renounced his
faith he would be a tyrant, and his hand would be the

more heavy and severe upon them. So it turned out.
Mosiy Schilo had them put in new chains, three to an
oar. The cruel fetters cut to the very bone; and he
beat them upon the back. But when the Turks,
rejoicing at having obtained such a servant, began to
carouse, and, forgetful of their law, all got drunk, he
distributed all the sixty-four keys among the prisoners,
in order that they might free themselves, fling their
chains and manacles into the sea, and, seizing their
swords, in turn kill the Turks. Then the Cossacks
collected great booty, and returned with glory to
their country; and the guitar-players celebrated Mosiy
Schilo's exploits for a long time. They would have
elected him Koschevoi, but he was a very eccentric
Cossack. At one time he would perform some feat
which the most sagacious would never have dreamed of.
At another, folly simply took possession of him, and he
drank and squandered everything away, was in debt
to every one in the Setch, and, in addition to that, stole
like a street thief. He carried off a whole Cossack
equipment from a strange kurén by night and pawned
it to the tavern-keeper. For this dishonourable act they
bound him to a post in the bazaar, and laid a club
beside him, in order that every one who passed should,
according to the measure of his strength, deal him a
blow. But there was not one Zaporozhetz out of them
all to be found who would raise the club against him,
remembering his former services. Such was the Cossack,
Mosiy Schilo.

" Here is one who will kill you, dog! " he said, springing upon the Lyakh. How they hacked away! their
shoulder-plates and breast-plates bent under their
blows. The hostile Lyakh cut through Schilo's shirt of
mail, reaching the body itself with his blade. The
Cossack's shirt was dyed purple: but Schilo heeded it
not. He brandished his brawny hand, heavy indeed
was that mighty fist, and brought the pommel of his
sword down unexpectedly upon his foeman's head.
The brazen helmet flew into pieces and the Lyakh

staggered and fell; but Schilo went on hacking and cutting gashes in the body of the stunned man. Kill not utterly thine enemy, Cossack: look back rather! The Cossack did not turn, and one of the dead man's servants plunged a knife into his neck. Schilo turned and tried to seize him, but he disappeared amid the smoke of the powder. On all sides rose the roar of matchlocks. Schilo knew that his wound was mortal. He fell with his hand upon his wound, and said, turning to his comrades, " Farewell, brother gentles, my comrades! may the holy Russian land stand forever, and may it be eternally honoured! " And as he closed his failing eyes, the Cossack soul fled from his grim body. Then Zadorozhniy came forward with his men, Vertikhvist issued from the ranks, and Balaban stepped forth.

" What now, gentles? " said Taras, calling to the hetmans by name: " there is yet powder in the powder-flasks? The Cossack force is not weakened? the Cossacks do not yield? "

" There is yet powder in the flasks, father; the Cossack force is not weakened yet: the Cossacks yield not! "

And the Cossacks pressed vigorously on: the foemen's ranks were disordered. The short colonel beat the assembly, and ordered eight painted standards to be displayed to collect his men, who were scattered over all the plain. All the Lyakhs hastened to the standards. But they had not yet succeeded in ranging themselves in order, when the hetman Kukubenko attacked their centre again with his Nezamáikovtzi and fell straight upon the stout colonel. The colonel could not resist the attack, and, wheeling his horse about, set out at a gallop; but Kukubenko pursued him for a considerable distance across the plain and prevented him from joining his regiment.

Perceiving this from the kurén on the flank, Stepan Guska set out after him, lasso in hand, bending his head to his horse's neck. Taking advantage of an opportunity,

he cast his lasso about his neck at the first attempt.
The colonel turned purple in the face, grasped the cord
with both hands, and tried to break it; but with a
powerful thrust Stepan drove his lance through his
body, and there he remained pinned to the earth. But
Guska did not escape his fate. The Cossacks had but
time to look round when they beheld Stepan Guska
elevated on four spears. All the poor fellow succeeded
in saying was, " May all our enemies perish, and may
the Russian land rejoice forever! " and then he yielded
up his soul.

The Cossacks glanced around, and there was Metélitza
on one side, entertaining the Lyakhs by dealing blows
on the head to one and another; on the other side, the
hetman Nevelitchkiy was attacking with his men; and
Zakrutibuga was repulsing and slaying the enemy by
the waggons. The third Pisarenko had repulsed a whole
squadron from the more distant waggons; and they
were still fighting and killing amongst the other
waggons, and even upon them.

" How now, gentles? " cried Taras, stepping forward
before them all: " is there still powder in your flasks?
Is the Cossack force still strong? do the Cossacks
yield? "

" There is still powder in the flasks, father; the
Cossack force is still strong: the Cossacks yield not! "

But Bovdug had already fallen from the waggons; a
bullet had struck him just below the heart. The old
man collected all his strength, and said, " I sorrow not
to part from the world. God grant every man such an
end! May the Russian land be forever glorious! " And
Bovdug's spirit flew above, to tell the old men who had
gone on long before that men still knew how to fight
on Russian soil, and better still, that they knew how to
die for it and the holy faith.

Balaban, hetman of a kurén, soon after fell to the
ground also from a waggon. Three mortal wounds had
ne received from a lance, a bullet, and a sword. He had
been one of the very best of Cossacks, and had accom-

plished a great deal as a commander on naval expeditions; but more glorious than all the rest was his raid on the shores of Anatolia. They collected many sequins, much valuable Turkish plunder, caftans, and adornments of every description. But misfortune awaited them on their way back. They came across the Turkish fleet, and were fired on by the ships. Half the boats were crushed and overturned, drowning more than one; but the bundles of reeds bound to the sides, Cossack fashion, saved the boats from completely sinking. Balaban rowed off at full speed, and steered straight in the face of the sun, thus rendering himself invisible to the Turkish ships. All the following night they spent in baling out the water with pails and their caps, and in repairing the damaged places. They made sails out of their Cossack trousers, and, sailing off, escaped from the fastest Turkish vessels. And not only did they arrive unharmed at the Setch, but they brought a gold-embroidered vesture for the archimandrite of the Mezhigorsky Monastery in Kief, and an ikon frame of pure silver for the church in honour of the Intercession of the Virgin Mary, which is in Zaporozhe. The guitar-players celebrated the daring of Balaban and his Cossacks for a long time afterwards. Now he bowed his head, feeling the pains which precede death, and said quietly, " I am permitted, brother gentles, to die a fine death. Seven have I hewn in pieces, nine have I pierced with my lance, many have I trampled upon with my horse's hoofs; and I no longer remember how many my bullets have slain. May our Russian land flourish forever! " and his spirit fled.

Cossacks, Cossacks! abandon not the flower of your army. Already was Kukubenko surrounded, and seven men only remained of all the Nezamaikovsky kurén, exhausted and with garments already stained with their blood. Taras himself, perceiving their straits, hastened to their rescue; but the Cossacks arrived too late. Before the enemies who surrounded him could be driven off, a spear was buried just below Kukubenko's heart.

He sank into the arms of the Cossacks who caught him, and his young blood flowed in a stream, like precious wine brought from the cellar in a glass vessel by careless servants, who, stumbling at the entrance, break the rich flask. The wine streams over the ground, and the master, hastening up, tears his hair, having reserved it, in order that if God should grant him, in his old age, to meet again the comrade of his youth, they might over it recall together former days, when a man enjoyed himself otherwise and better than now. Kukubenko cast his eyes around, and said, " I thank God that it has been my lot to die before your eyes, comrades. May they live better who come after us than we have lived; and may our Russian land, beloved by Christ, flourish forever! " and his young spirit fled. The angels took it in their arms and bore it to heaven: it will be well with him there. " Sit down at my right hand, Kukubenko," Christ will say to him: " you never betrayed your comrades, you never committed a dishonourable act, you never sold a man into misery, you preserved and defended my church." The death of Kukubenko saddened them all. The Cossack ranks were terribly thinned. Many brave men were missing, but the Cossacks still stood their ground.

" How now, gentles? " cried Taras to the remaining kuréns: " is there still powder in your flasks? Are your swords blunted? Are the Cossack forces wearied? Have the Cossacks given way? "

" There is still an abundance of powder; our swords are still sharp; the Cossack forces are not wearied, and the Cossacks have not yet yielded."

And the Cossacks again strained every nerve, as though they had suffered no loss. Only three kurén hetmans still remained alive. Red blood flowed in streams everywhere; heaps of their bodies and of those of the enemy were piled high. Taras looked up to heaven, and there already hovered a flock of vultures. Well, there would be prey for some one. And there the foe were raising Metélitza on their lances, and the head of the second Pisarenko was dizzily opening and shutting its eyes; and the mangled body of Okhrim Guska fell upon the ground. "Now," said Taras, and waved a cloth on high. Ostap understood this signal and springing quickly from his ambush attacked sharply. The Lyakhs could not withstand this onslaught; and he drove them back, and chased them straight to the spot where the stakes and fragments of spears were driven into the earth. The horses began to stumble and fall and the Lyakhs to fly over their heads. At that moment the Korsuntzi, who had stood till the last by the baggage waggons, perceived that they still had some bullets left, and suddenly fired a volley from their matchlocks. The Lyakhs became confused, and lost their presence of mind; and the Cossacks took courage. "The victory is ours!" rang Cossack voices on all sides; the trumpets sounded and the banner of victory was unfurled. The beaten Lyakhs ran in all directions and hid themselves. "No, the victory is not yet complete," said Taras, glancing at the city gate; and he was right.

The gates opened, and out dashed a hussar band, the flower of all the cavalry. Every rider was mounted on a matched brown horse from the Kabardei; and in front rode the handsomest, the most heroic of them all. His black hair streamed from beneath his brazen helmet; and from his arm floated a rich scarf, embroidered by the hands of a peerless beauty. Taras sprang back in horror when he saw that it was Andrii. And the latter meanwhile, enveloped in the dust and heat of battle, eager to deserve the scarf which had been bound as a gift upon his arm, flew on like a greyhound; the handsomest, most agile, and youngest of all the band. The experienced huntsman urges on the greyhound, and he springs forward, tossing up the snow, and a score of times outrunning the hare, in the ardour of his course. And so it was with Andrii. Old Taras paused and observed how he cleared a path before him, hewing away and dealing blows to the right and the left. Taras

E 1740

could not restrain himself, but shouted: " Your comrades! your comrades! you devil's brat, would you kill your own comrades? " But Andríi distinguished not who stood before him, comrades or strangers; he saw nothing. Curls, long curls, were what he saw; and a bosom like that of a river swan, and a snowy neck and shoulders, and all that is created for rapturous kisses.

" Hey there, lads! only draw him to the forest, entice him to the forest for me! " shouted Taras. Instantly thirty of the smartest Cossacks volunteered to entice him thither; and settling their tall caps firmly, spurred their horses straight at a gap in the hussars. They attacked the front ranks in flank, beat them down, cut them off from the rear ranks, and slew many of them. Golopuitenko struck Andríi on the back with his sword, and immediately set out to ride away at the top of his speed. How Andríi flew after him! How his young blood coursed through all his veins! Driving his sharp spurs into his horse's flanks, he tore along after the Cossacks, never glancing back, and not perceiving that only twenty men at the most were following him. The Cossacks fled at full gallop, and directed their course straight for the forest. Andríi overtook them, and was on the point of catching Golopuitenko, when a powerful hand seized his horse's bridle. Andríi looked; before him stood Taras! He trembled all over, and turned suddenly pale, like a student who, receiving a blow on the forehead with a ruler, flushes up like fire, springs in wrath from his seat to chase his comrade, and suddenly encounters his teacher entering the classroom; in an instant his wrathful impulse calms down and his futile anger vanishes. In this wise, in an instant, Andríi's wrath was as if it had never existed. And he beheld before him only his terrible father.

" Well, what are we going to do now? " said Taras, looking him straight in the eyes. But Andríi could make no reply to this, and stood with his eyes fixed on the ground.

" Well, son; did your Lyakhs help you? "

Andríi made no answer.

" To think that you should be such a traitor! that you should betray your faith! betray your comrades! Dismount from your horse! "

Obedient as a child, he dismounted, and stood before Taras more dead than alive.

" Stand still, do not move! I gave you life, I will also kill you! " said Taras, and, retreating a step backwards, he brought his gun up to his shoulder. Andríi was white as a sheet; his lips moved gently, and he uttered a name; but it was not the name of his native land, nor of his mother, nor his brother; it was the name of the beautiful Pole. Taras fired.

Like the ear of corn cut down by the reaping-hook, like the young lamb when it feels the deadly steel in its heart, he hung his head and rolled upon the grass without uttering a word.

The murderer of his son stood still, and gazed long upon the lifeless body. Even in death he was very handsome; his manly face, so short a time ago filled with power, and with an irresistible charm for every woman, still had a marvellous beauty; his black brows, like sombre velvet, set off his pale features.

" Is he not a true Cossack? " said Taras; " he is tall of stature, and black-browed, his face is that of a noble, and his hand was strong in battle! He is fallen! fallen without glory, like a vile dog! "

" Father, what have you done? Was it you who killed him? " said Ostap, coming up at this moment.

Taras nodded.

Ostap gazed intently at the dead man. He was sorry for his brother, and said at once: " Let us give him honourable burial, father, that the foe may not dishonour his body, nor the birds of prey rend it."

" They will bury him without our help," said Taras; " there will be plenty of mourners and rejoicers for him."

And he reflected for a couple of minutes, whether he should fling him to the wolves for prey, or respect in

him the bravery which every brave man is bound to
honour in another, no matter whom? Then he saw
Golopuitenko galloping towards them and crying:
" Woe, hetman, the Lyakhs have been reinforced, a
fresh force has come to their rescue! " Golopuitenko had
not finished speaking when Vovtuzenko galloped up:
" Woe, hetman! a fresh force is bearing down upon us."

Vovtuzenko had not finished speaking when Pisarenko rushed up without his horse: " Where are you,
father? The Cossacks are seeking for you. Hetman
Nevelitchkiy is killed, Zadorozhniy is killed, and
Tcherevitchenko: but the Cossacks stand their ground;
they will not die without looking in your eyes; they
want you to gaze upon them once more before the hour
of death arrives."

" To horse, Ostap! " said Taras, and hastened to
find his Cossacks, to look once more upon them, and let
them behold their hetman once more before the hour of
death. But before they could emerge from the wood,
the enemy's force had already surrounded it on all sides,
and horsemen armed with swords and spears appeared
everywhere between the trees. " Ostap, Ostap! don't
yield! " shouted Taras, and grasping his sword he began
to cut down all he encountered on every side. But six
suddenly sprang upon Ostap. They did it in an unpro-
pitious hour: the head of one flew off, another turned
to flee, a spear pierced the ribs of a third; a fourth,
more bold, bent his head to escape the bullet, and the
bullet striking his horse's breast, the maddened animal
reared, fell back upon the earth, and crushed his rider
under him. " Well done, son! Well done, Ostap! " cried
Taras: " I am following you." And he drove off those
who attacked him. Taras hewed and fought, dealing
blows at one after another, but still keeping his eye
upon Ostap ahead. He saw that eight more were falling
upon his son. " Ostap, Ostap! don't yield! " But they
had already overpowered Ostap; one had flung his
lasso about his neck, and they had bound him, and
were carrying him away. " Hey, Ostap, Ostap! "

shouted Taras, forcing his way towards him, and cutting
men down like cabbages to right and left. "Hey,
Ostap, Ostap!" But something at that moment struck
him like a heavy stone. All grew dim and confused
before his eyes. In one moment there flashed confusedly
before him heads, spears, smoke, the gleam of fire, tree-
trunks, and leaves; and then he sank heavily to the
earth like a felled oak, and darkness covered his eyes.

X

"I HAVE slept a long while!" said Taras, coming to his
senses, as if after a heavy drunken sleep, and trying to
distinguish the objects about him. A terrible weakness
overpowered his limbs. The walls and corners of a
strange room were dimly visible before him. At length
he perceived that Tovkatch was seated beside him,
apparently listening to his every breath.

"Yes," thought Tovkatch, "you might have slept
forever." But he said nothing, only shook his finger,
and motioned him to be silent.

"But tell me where I am now?" asked Taras,
straining his mind, and trying to recollect what had
taken place.

"Be silent!" cried his companion sternly. "Why
should you want to know? Don't you see that you are
all hacked to pieces? Here I have been galloping with
you for two weeks without taking breath; and you
have been burnt up with fever and talking nonsense.
This is the first time you have slept quietly. Be silent
if you don't wish to do yourself an injury."

But Taras still tried to collect his thoughts and to
recall what had passed. "Well, the Lyakhs must have
surrounded and captured me. I had no chance of
fighting my way clear from the throng."

"Be silent, I tell you, you devil's brat!" cried
Tovkatch angrily, as a nurse, driven beyond her patience, cries out at her unruly charge. "What good will

it do you to know how you got away? It is enough that
you did get away. Some people were found who would
not abandon you; let that be enough for you. It is
something for me to have ridden all night with you.
You think that you passed for a common Cossack?
No, they have offered a reward of two thousand ducats
for your head."

"And Ostap!" cried Taras suddenly, and tried to
rise; for all at once he recollected that Ostap had been
seized and bound before his very eyes, and that he was
now in the hands of the Lyakhs. Grief overpowered him.
He pulled off and tore in pieces the bandages from his
wounds, and threw them far from him; he tried to say
something, but only articulated some incoherent words.
Fever and delirium seized upon him afresh, and he
uttered wild and incoherent speeches. Meanwhile his
faithful comrade stood beside him, scolding and shower-
ing harsh, reproachful words upon him without stint.
Finally he seized him by the arms and legs, wrapped
him up like a child, arranged all his bandages, rolled
him in an ox-hide, bound him with bast, and, fastening
him with ropes to his saddle, rode with him again at full
speed along the road.

"I'll get you there, even if it be not alive! I will not
abandon you for the Lyakhs to make merry over you,
and cut your body in twain and fling it into the water.
Let the eagle tear out your eyes if it must be so; but let
it be our eagle of the steppe and not a Polish eagle, not
one which has flown hither from Polish soil. I will
bring you, though it be a corpse, to the Ukraine!"

Thus spoke his faithful companion. He rode without
drawing rein, day and night, and brought Taras still
insensible into the Zaporozhian Setch itself. There he
undertook to cure him, with unswerving care, by the
aid of herbs and liniments. He sought out a skilful
Jewess, who made Taras drink various potions for a
whole month, and at length he improved. Whether it
was owing to the medicine or to his iron constitution
gaining the upper hand, at all events, in six weeks he

was on his feet. His wounds had closed, and only the scars of the sabre-cuts showed how deeply injured the old Cossack had been. But he was markedly sad and morose. Three deep wrinkles engraved themselves upon his brow and never more departed thence. Then he looked around him. All was new in the Setch; all his old companions were dead. Not one was left of those who had stood up for the right, for faith and brotherhood. And those who had gone forth with the Koschevoi in pursuit of the Tatars, they also had long since disappeared. All had perished. One had lost his head in battle; another had died for lack of food, amid the salt marshes of the Crimea; another had fallen in captivity and been unable to survive the disgrace. Their former Koschevoi was no longer living, nor any of his old companions, and the grass was growing over those once alert with power. He felt as one who had given a feast, a great noisy feast. All the dishes had been smashed in pieces; not a drop of wine was left anywhere; the guests and servants had all stolen valuable cups and platters; and he, like the master of the house, stood sadly thinking that it would have been no feast. In vain did they try to cheer Taras and to divert his mind; in vain did the long-bearded, grey-haired guitar-players come by twos and threes to glorify his Cossack deeds. He gazed grimly and indifferently at everything, with inappeasable grief printed on his stolid face; and said softly, as he drooped his head, " My son, my Ostap! "

The Zaporozhtzi assembled for a raid by sea. Two hundred boats were launched on the Dnieper, and Asia Minor saw those who manned them, with their shaven heads and long scalp-locks, devote her thriving shores to fire and sword; she saw the turbans of her Mahometan inhabitants strewn, like her innumerable flowers, over the blood-besprinkled fields, and floating along her river banks; she saw many tarry Zaporozhian trousers, and strong hands with black hunting-whips. The Zaporozhtzi ate up and laid waste all the vineyards.

In the mosques they left heaps of dung. They used rich Persian shawls for sashes, and girded their dirty gaberdines with them. Long afterwards, short Zaporozhian pipes were found in those regions. They sailed merrily back. A ten-gun Turkish ship pursued them and scattered their skiffs, like birds, with a volley from its guns. A third part of them sank in the depths of the sea; but the rest again assembled, and gained the mouth of the Dnieper with twelve kegs full of sequins. But all this did not interest Taras. He went off upon the steppe as though to hunt; but the charge remained in his gun, and, laying down the weapon, he would seat himself sadly on the shores of the sea. He sat there long with drooping head, repeating continually, " My Ostap, my Ostap! " Before him spread the gleaming Black Sea; in the distant reeds the sea-gull screamed. His grey moustache turned to silver, and the tears fell one by one upon it.

At last Taras could endure it no longer. " Whatever happens, I must go and find out what he is doing. Is he alive, or in the grave? I will know, cost what it may! " Within a week he found himself in the city of Ouman, fully armed, and mounted, with lance, sword, canteen, pot of oatmeal, powder horn, cord to hobble his horse, and other equipments. He went straight to a dirty, ill-kept little house, the small windows of which were almost invisible, blackened as they were with some unknown dirt. The chimney was wrapped in rags; and the roof, which was full of holes, was covered with sparrows. A heap of all sorts of refuse lay before the very door. From the window peered the head of a Jewess, in a head-dress with discoloured pearls.

" Is your husband at home? " said Bulba, dismounting, and fastening his horse's bridle to an iron hook beside the door.

" He is at home," said the Jewess, and hastened out at once with a measure of corn for the horse, and a stoup of beer for the rider.

" Where is your Jew? "

" He is in the other room at prayer," replied the Jewess, bowing and wishing Bulba good health as he raised the cup to his lips.

" Remain here, feed and water my horse, whilst I go speak with him alone. I have business with him."

This Jew was the well-known Yankel. He was there as revenue-farmer and tavern-keeper. He had gradually got nearly all the neighbouring noblemen and gentlemen into his hands, had slowly sucked away most of their money, and had strongly impressed his presence on that locality. For a distance of three miles in all directions, not a single farm remained in a proper state. All were falling in ruins; all had been drunk away, and poverty and rags alone remained. The whole neighbourhood was depopulated, as if after a fire or an epidemic; and if Yankel had lived there ten years, he would probably have depopulated the Waiwode's whole domains.

Taras entered the room. The Jew was praying, enveloped in his dirty shroud, and was turning to spit for the last time, according to the forms of his creed, when his eye suddenly lighted on Taras standing behind him. The first thing that crossed Yankel's mind was the two thousand ducats offered for his visitor's head; but he was ashamed of his avarice, and tried to stifle within him the eternal thought of gold, which twines, like a snake, about the soul of a Jew.

" Listen, Yankel," said Taras to the Jew, who began to bow low before him, and as he spoke he shut the door so that they might not be seen, " I saved your life: the Zaporozhtzi would have torn you in pieces like a dog. Now it is your turn to do me a service."

The Jew's face clouded over a little.

" What service? If it is a service I can render, why should not I render it? "

" Ask no questions. Take me to Warsaw."

" To Warsaw? Why to Warsaw? " said the Jew, and his brows and shoulders rose in amazement.

" Ask me nothing. Take me to Warsaw. I must see him once more at any cost, and say one word to him."

" Say a word to whom? "

" To him—to Ostap—to my son."

" Has not my lord heard that already——"

" I know, I know all. They offer two thousand ducats for my head. They know its value, fools! I will give you five thousand. Here are two thousand on the spot," and Bulba poured out two thousand ducats from a leather purse, " and the rest when I return."

The Jew instantly seized a towel and concealed the ducats under it. " Ai, glorious money! ai, good money!" he said, twirling one gold piece in his hand and testing it with his teeth. " I don't believe the man from whom my lord took these fine gold pieces remained in the world an hour longer; he went straight to the river and drowned himself, after the loss of such magnificent gold pieces."

" I should not have asked you, I might possibly have found my own way to Warsaw; but some one might recognise me, and then the cursed Lyakhs would capture me, for I am not clever at inventions; whilst that is just what you Jews are created for. You would deceive the very devil. You know every trick: that is why I have come to you; and, besides, I could do nothing of myself in Warsaw. Harness the horse to your waggon at once and take me."

" And my lord thinks that I can take the nag at once, and harness him, and say ' Get up, Dapple!' My lord thinks that I can take him just as he is, without concealing him? "

" Well, hide me, hide me as you like: in an empty cask? "

" Ai, ai! and my lord thinks he can be concealed in an empty cask? Does not my lord know that every man thinks that every cask he sees contains brandy? "

" Well, let them think it is brandy."

" Let them think it is brandy? " said the Jew, and grasped his ear-locks with both hands, and then raised them both on high.

" Well, why are you so frightened? "

"And does not my lord know that God has made brandy expressly for every one to sip? They are all gluttons and fond of dainties there: a nobleman will run five versts after a cask; he will make a hole in it, and as soon as he sees that nothing runs out, he will say, 'A Jew does not carry empty casks; there is certainly something wrong. Seize the Jew, bind the Jew, take away all the Jew's money, put the Jew in prison!' Then all the vile people will fall upon the Jew, for every one takes a Jew for a dog; and they think he is not a man, but only a Jew."

"Then put me in the waggon with some fish over me."

"I cannot, my lord, by heaven, I cannot: all over Poland the people are as hungry as dogs now. They will steal the fish, and feel my lord."

"Then take me in the fiend's way, only take me."

"Listen, listen, my lord!" said the Jew, turning up the ends of his sleeves, and approaching him with extended arms. "This is what we will do. They are building fortresses and castles everywhere: French engineers have come from Germany, and so a great deal of brick and stone is being carried over the roads. Let my lord lie down in the bottom of the waggon, and over him I will pile bricks. My lord is strong and well, apparently, so he will not mind if it is a little heavy; and I will make a hole in the bottom of the waggon in order to feed my lord."

"Do what you will, only take me!"

In an hour, a waggon-load of bricks left Ouman, drawn by two sorry nags. On one of them sat tall Yankel, his long, curling ear-locks flowing from beneath his Jewish cap, as he bounced about on the horse, like a verst-mark planted by the roadside.

XI

AT the time when these things took place, there were as
yet on the frontiers neither custom-house officials nor
guards—those bugbears of enterprising people—so that
any one could bring across anything he fancied. If any
one made a search or inspection, he did it chiefly for his
own pleasure, especially if there happened to be in the
waggon objects attractive to his eye, and if his own
hand possessed a certain weight and power. But the
bricks found no admirers, and they entered the principal
gate unmolested. Bulba, in his narrow cage, could only
hear the noise, the shouts of the driver, and nothing
more. Yankel, bouncing up and down on his dust-covered
nag, turned, after making several *détours*, into a dark,
narrow street bearing the names of the Muddy and also
of the Jews' Street, because Jews from nearly every
part of Warsaw were to be found here. This street
greatly resembled a back-yard turned wrong side out.
The sun never seemed to shine into it. The black
wooden houses, with numerous poles projecting from
the windows, still further increased the darkness.
Rarely did a brick wall gleam red among them; for
these too, in many places, had turned quite black.
Here and there, high up, a bit of stuccoed wall illumined by the sun glistened with intolerable whiteness.
Pipes, rags, shells, broken and discarded tubs: every
one flung whatever was useless to him into the street,
thus affording the passer-by an opportunity of exercising all his five senses with the rubbish. A man on
horseback could almost touch with his hand the poles
thrown across the street from one house to another,
upon which hung Jewish stockings, short trousers, and
smoked geese. Sometimes a pretty little Hebrew face,
adorned with discoloured pearls, peeped out of an old
window. A group of little Jews, with torn and dirty
garments and curly hair, screamed and rolled about in

the dirt. A red-haired Jew, with freckles all over his face which made him look like a sparrow's egg, gazed from a window. He addressed Yankel at once in his gibberish, and Yankel at once drove into a court-yard. Another Jew came along, halted, and entered into conversation. When Bulba finally emerged from beneath the bricks, he beheld three Jews talking with great warmth.

Yankel turned to him and said that everything possible would be done; that his Ostap was in the city jail, and that although it would be difficult to persuade the jailer, yet he hoped to arrange a meeting.

Bulba entered the room with the three Jews.

The Jews again began to talk among themselves in their incomprehensible tongue. Taras looked hard at each of them. Something seemed to have moved him deeply; over his rough and stolid countenance a flame of hope spread, of hope such as sometimes visits a man in the last depths of despair; his aged heart began to beat violently as though he had been a youth.

" Listen, Jews! " said he, and there was a triumphant ring in his words. " You can do anything in the world, even extract things from the bottom of the sea; and it has long been a proverb, that a Jew will steal from himself if he takes a fancy to steal. Set my Ostap at liberty! give him a chance to escape from their diabolical hands. I promised this man five thousand ducats; I will add another five thousand: all that I have, rich cups, buried gold, houses, all, even to my last garment, I will part with; and I will enter into a contract with you for my whole life, to give you half of all the booty I may gain in war."

" Oh, impossible, dear lord, it is impossible! " said Yankel with a sigh.

" Impossible," said another Jew.

All three Jews looked at each other.

" We might try," said the third, glancing timidly at the other two. " God may favour us."

All three Jews discussed the matter in German.

Bulba, in spite of his straining his ears, could make nothing of it; he only caught the word *Mardokhai* often repeated.

"Listen, my lord!" said Yankel. "We must consult with a man such as there never was before in the world . . . ugh, ugh! as wise as Solomon; and if he will do nothing, then no one in the world can. Sit here: this is the key; admit no one." The Jews went out into the street.

Taras locked the door, and looked out from the little window upon the dirty Jewish street. The three Jews halted in the middle of the street and began to talk with a good deal of warmth: a fourth soon joined them, and finally a fifth. Again he heard repeated, *Mardokhai, Mardokhai!* The Jews glanced incessantly towards one side of the street; at length from a dirty house near the end of it emerged a foot in a Jewish shoe and the skirts of a caftan. "Ah! Mardokhai, Mardokhai!" shouted the Jews in one voice. A thin Jew somewhat shorter than Yankel, but even more wrinkled, and with a huge upper lip, approached the impatient group; and all the Jews made haste to talk to him, interrupting each other. During the recital, Mardokhai glanced several times towards the little window, and Taras divined that the conversation concerned him.

Mardokhai waved his hands, listened, interrupted, spat frequently to one side, and, pulling up the skirts of his caftan, thrust his hand into his pocket and drew out some jingling thing, showing very dirty trousers in the operation. Finally all the Jews set up such a shouting that the Jew who was standing guard was forced to make a signal for silence, and Taras began to fear for his safety; but when he remembered that Jews can only consult in the street, and that the devil himself cannot understand their language, he regained his composure.

Two minutes later the Jews all entered the room together. Mardokhai approached Taras, tapped him on the shoulder, and said, "When we set to work it will

be all right." Taras looked at this Solomon whom the
world had never known and conceived some hope:
indeed, his face might well inspire confidence. His upper
lip was simply an object of horror; its thickness being
doubtless increased by adventitious circumstances.
This Solomon's beard consisted only of about fifteen
hairs, and they were on the left side. Solomon's face
bore so many scars of battle, received for his daring,
that he had doubtless lost count of them long before,
and had grown accustomed to consider them as birth-
marks.

Mardokhai departed, accompanied by his comrades,
who were filled with admiration at his wisdom. Bulba
remained alone. He was in a strange, unaccustomed
situation for the first time in his life; he felt uneasy.
His mind was in a state of fever. He was no longer
unbending, immovable, strong as an oak, as he had
formerly been: but felt timid and weak. He trembled
at every sound, at every fresh Jewish face which showed
itself at the end of the street. In this condition he passed
the whole day. He neither ate nor drank, and his eye
never for a moment left the small window looking on
the street. Finally, late at night, Mardokhai and Yankel
made their appearance. Taras's heart died within
him.

"What news? have you been successful?" he asked
with the impatience of a wild horse.

But before the Jews had recovered breath to answer,
Taras perceived that Mardokhai no longer had the
locks, which had formerly fallen in greasy curls from
under his felt cap. It was evident that he wished to say
something, but he uttered only nonsense which Taras
could make nothing of. Yankel himself put his hand
very often to his mouth as though suffering from a
cold.

"Oh, dearest lord!" said Yankel: "it is quite
impossible now! by heaven, impossible! Such vile
people that they deserve to be spat upon! Mardokhai
here says the same. Mardokhai has done what no man

in the world ever did, but God did not will that it should be so. Three thousand soldiers are in garrison here, and to-morrow the prisoners are all to be executed."

Taras looked the Jew straight in the face, but no longer with impatience or anger.

"But if my lord wishes to see his son, then it must be early to-morrow morning, before the sun has risen. The sentinels have consented, and one gaoler has promised. But may he have no happiness in the world, woe is me! What greedy people! There are none such among us: I gave fifty ducats to each sentinel and to the gaoler."

"Good. Take me to him!" exclaimed Taras, with decision, and with all his firmness of mind restored. He agreed to Yankel's proposition that he should disguise himself as a foreign count, just arrived from Germany, for which purpose the prudent Jew had already provided a costume. It was already night. The master of the house, the red-haired Jew with freckles, pulled out a mattress covered with some kind of a rug, and spread it on a bench for Bulba. Yankel lay upon the floor on a similar mattress. The red-haired Jew drank a small cup of brandy, took off his caftan, and betook himself—looking, in his shoes and stockings, very like a lean chicken—with his wife, to something resembling a cupboard. Two little Jews lay down on the floor beside the cupboard, like a couple of dogs. But Taras did not sleep; he sat motionless, drumming on the table with his fingers. He kept his pipe in his mouth, and puffed out smoke, which made the Jew sneeze in his sleep and pull his coverlet over his nose. Scarcely was the sky touched with the first faint gleams of dawn than he pushed Yankel with his foot, saying: "Rise, Jew, and give me your count's dress!"

In a moment he was dressed. He blackened his moustache and eyebrows, put on his head a small dark cap; even the Cossacks who knew him best would not have recognised him. Apparently he was not more than thirty-five. A healthy colour glowed on his cheeks, and his scars lent him an air of command. The gold-embroidered dress became him extremely well.

The streets were still asleep. Not a single one of the market folk as yet showed himself in the city, with his basket on his arm. Yankel and Bulba made their way to a building which presented the appearance of a crouching stork. It was large, low, wide, and black; and on one side a long slender tower like a stork's neck projected above the roof. This building served for a variety of purposes; it was a barrack, a jail, and the criminal court. The visitors entered the gate and found themselves in a vast room, or covered courtyard. About a thousand men were sleeping here. Straight before them was a small door, in front of which sat two sentries playing at some game which consisted in one striking the palm of the other's hand with two fingers. They paid little heed to the new arrivals, and only turned their heads when Yankel said, " It is we, sirs; do you hear? it is we."

" Go in! " said one of them, opening the door with one hand, and holding out the other to his comrade to receive his blows.

They entered a low and dark corridor, which led them to a similar room with small windows overhead. " Who goes there? " shouted several voices, and Taras beheld a number of warriors in full armour. " We have been ordered to admit no one."

" It is we! " cried Yankel; " we, by heavens, noble sirs! " But no one would listen to him. Fortunately, at that moment a fat man came up, who appeared to be a commanding officer, for he swore louder than all the others.

" My lord, it is we! you know us, and the lord count will thank you."

" Admit them, a hundred fiends, and mother of fiends! Admit no one else. And no one is to draw his sword, nor quarrel."

The conclusion of this order the visitors did not hear. " It is we, it is I, it is your friends! " Yankel said to every one they met.

" Well, can it be managed now? " he inquired of one
of the guards, when they at length reached the end of
the corridor.

" It is possible, but I don't know whether you will be
able to gain admission to the prison itself. Yana is not
here now; another man is keeping watch in his place,"
replied the guard.

" Ai, ai! " cried the Jew softly: " this is bad, my
dear lord! "

" Go on! " said Taras, firmly, and the Jew obeyed.

At the arched entrance of the vaults stood a heyduke,
with a moustache trimmed in three layers: the upper
layer was trained backwards, the second straight
forward, and the third downwards, which made him
greatly resemble a cat.

The Jew shrank into nothing and approached him
almost sideways: " Your high excellency! High and
illustrious lord! "

" Are you speaking to me, Jew? "

" To you, illustrious lord."

" Hm, but I am merely a heyduke," said the merry-
eyed man with the triple-tiered moustache.

" And I thought it was the Waiwode himself, by
heavens! Ai, ai, ai! " Thereupon the Jew twisted his
head about and spread out his fingers. " Ai, what a
fine figure! Another finger's-breadth and he would be a
colonel. The lord no doubt rides a horse as fleet as the
wind and commands the troops! "

The heyduke twirled the lower tier of his moustache,
and his eyes beamed.

" What a warlike people! " continued the Jew. " Ah,
woe is me, what a fine race! Golden cords and trappings
that shine like the sun; and the maidens, wherever they
see warriors—Ai, ai! " Again the Jew wagged his head.

The heyduke twirled his upper moustache and
uttered a sound somewhat resembling the neighing of a
horse.

" I pray my lord to do us a service! " exclaimed the
Jew: " this prince has come hither from a foreign land,

and wants to get a look at the Cossacks. He never, in all his life, has seen what sort of people the Cossacks are."

The advent of foreign counts and barons was common enough in Poland: they were often drawn thither by curiosity to view this half-Asiatic corner of Europe. They regarded Moscow and the Ukraine as situated in Asia. So the heyduke bowed low, and thought fit to add a few words of his own.

"I do not know, your excellency," said he, "why you should desire to see them. They are dogs, not men; and their faith is such as no one respects."

"You lie, you son of Satan!" exclaimed Bulba. "You are a dog yourself! How dare you say that our faith is not respected? It is your heretical faith which is not respected."

"Oho!" said the heyduke. "I can guess who you are, my friend; you are one of the breed of those under my charge. So just wait while I summon our men."

Taras realised his indiscretion, but vexation and obstinacy hindered him from devising a means of remedying it. Fortunately Yankel managed to interpose at this moment:—

"Most noble lord, how is it possible that the count can be a Cossack? If he were a Cossack, where could have he obtained such a dress, and such a count-like mien?"

"Explain that yourself." And the heyduke opened his wide mouth to shout.

"Your royal highness, silence, silence, for heaven's sake!" cried Yankel. "Silence! we will pay you for it in a way you never dreamed of: we will give you two golden ducats."

"Oho! two ducats! I can't do anything with two ducats. I give my barber two ducats for only shaving the half of my beard. Give me a hundred ducats, Jew." Here the heyduke twirled his upper moustache. "If you don't, I will shout at once."

"Why so much?" said the Jew, sadly, turning pale, and undoing his leather purse; but it was lucky that he had no more in it, and that the heyduke could not count over a hundred.

" My lord, my lord, let us depart quickly! Look at the evil-minded fellow! " said Yankel to Taras, perceiving that the heyduke was turning the money over in his hand, as though regretting that he had not demanded more.

" What do you mean, you devil of a heyduke? " said Bulba. " What do you mean by taking our money and not letting us see the Cossacks? No, you must let us see them. Since you have taken the money, you have no right to refuse."

" Go, go to the devil! If you won't, I'll give the alarm this moment. Take yourselves off quickly, I say! "

" My lord, my lord, let us go! in God's name let us go! Curse him! May he dream such things that he will have to spit," cried poor Yankel.

Bulba turned slowly, with drooping head, and retraced his steps, followed by the complaints of Yankel, who was sorrowing at the thought of the wasted ducats.

" Why be angry? Let the dog curse. That race cannot help cursing. Oh, woe is me, what luck God sends to some people! A hundred ducats merely for driving us off! And our brother: they have torn off his ear-locks, and they made wounds on his face that you cannot bear to look at, and yet no one will give him a hundred gold pieces. O heavens! Merciful God! "

But this failure made a much deeper impression on Bulba, expressed by a devouring flame in his eyes.

" Let us go," he said, suddenly, as if arousing himself; " let us go to the square. I want to see how they will torture him."

" Oh, my lord! why go? That will do us no good now."

" Let us go," said Bulba, obstinately; and the Jew followed him, sighing like a nurse.

The square on which the execution was to take place was not hard to find: for the people were thronging

thither from all quarters. In that savage age such a
thing constituted one of the most noteworthy spec-
tacles, not only for the common people, but among the
higher classes. A number of the most pious old men, a
throng of young girls, and the most cowardly women,
who dreamed the whole night afterwards of bloody
corpses, and shrieked as loudly in their sleep as a
drunken hussar, missed, nevertheless, no opportunity
of gratifying their curiosity. " Ah, what tortures! "
many of them would cry, hysterically, covering their
eyes and turning away; but they stood their ground
for a good while, all the same. Many a one, with gaping
mouth and outstretched hands, would have liked to
jump upon other folk's heads, to get a better view.
Above the crowd towered a bulky butcher, admiring
the whole process with the air of a connoisseur, and
exchanging brief remarks with a gunsmith, whom he
addressed as " Gossip," because he got drunk in the
same alehouse with him on holidays. Some entered into
warm discussions, others even laid wagers. But the
majority were of the species who, all the world over,
look on at the world and at everything that goes on in
it and merely scratch their noses. In the front ranks,
close to the bearded civic-guards, stood a young noble,
in warlike array, who had certainly put his whole
wardrobe on his back, leaving only his torn shirt and old
shoes at his quarters. Two chains, one above the other,
hung around his neck. He stood beside his mistress,
Usisya, and glanced about incessantly to see that no
one soiled her silk gown. He explained everything to
her so perfectly that no one could have added a word.
" All these people whom you see, my dear Usisya," he
said, " have come to see the criminals executed; and
that man, my love, yonder, holding the axe and other
instruments in his hands, is the executioner, who will
despatch them. When he begins to break them on the
wheel, and torture them in other ways, the criminals
will be still alive; but when he cuts off their heads,
then, my love, they will die at once. Before that, they

will cry and move; but as soon as their heads are cut off, it will be impossible for them to cry, or to eat or drink, because, my dear, they will no longer have any head." Usisya listened to all this with terror and curiosity.

The upper stories of the houses were filled with people. From the windows in the roof peered strange faces with beards and something resembling caps. Upon the balconies, beneath shady awnings, sat the aristocracy. The hands of smiling young ladies, brilliant as white sugar, rested on the railings. Portly nobles looked on with dignity. Servants in rich garb, with flowing sleeves, handed round various refreshments. Sometimes a black-eyed young rogue would take her cake or fruit and fling it among the crowd with her own noble little hand. The crowd of hungry gentles held up their caps to receive it; and some tall noble, whose head rose amid the throng, with his faded red jacket and discoloured gold braid, and who was the first to catch it with the aid of his long arms, would kiss his booty, press it to his heart, and finally put it in his mouth. The hawk, suspended beneath the balcony in a golden cage, was also a spectator; with beak inclined to one side, and with one foot raised, he, too, watched the people attentively. But suddenly a murmur ran through the crowd, and a rumour spread, " They are coming! they are coming! the Cossacks! "

They were bare-headed, with their long locks floating in the air. Their beards had grown, and their once handsome garments were worn out, and hung about them in tatters. They walked neither timidly nor surlily, but with a certain pride, neither looking at nor bowing to the people. At the head of all came Ostap.

What were old Taras's feelings when thus he beheld his Ostap? What filled his heart then? He gazed at him from amid the crowd, and lost not a single movement of his. They reached the place of execution. Ostap stopped. He was to be the first to drink the bitter cup. He glanced at his comrades, raised his hand, and said in a loud voice: " God grant that none of the heretics who stand here may hear, the unclean dogs, how Christians suffer! Let none of us utter a single word." After this he ascended the scaffold.

" Well done, son! well done! " said Bulba, softly, and bent his grey head.

The executioner tore off his old rags; they fastened his hands and feet in stocks prepared expressly, and——
We will not pain the reader with a picture of the hellish tortures which would make his hair rise upright on his head. They were the outcome of that coarse, wild age, when men still led a life of warfare which hardened their souls until no sense of humanity was left in them. In vain did some, not many, in that age make a stand against such terrible measures. In vain did the king and many nobles, enlightened in mind and spirit, demonstrate that such severity of punishment could but fan the flame of vengeance in the Cossack nation. But the power of the king, and the opinion of the wise, was as nothing before the savage will of the magnates of the kingdom, who, by their thoughtlessness and unconquerable lack of all far-sighted policy, their childish self-love and miserable pride, converted the Diet into the mockery of a government. Ostap endured the torture like a giant. Not a cry, not a groan, was heard. Even when they began to break the bones in his hands and feet, when, amid the death-like stillness of the crowd, the horrible cracking was audible to the most distant spectators; when even his tormentors turned aside their eyes, nothing like a groan escaped his lips, nor did his face quiver. Taras stood in the crowd with bowed head; and, raising his eyes proudly at that moment, he said, approvingly, " Well done, boy! well done! "

But when they took him to the last deadly tortures, it seemed as though his strength were failing. He cast his eyes around.

O God! all strangers, all unknown faces! If only some of his relatives had been present at his death! He would not have cared to hear the sobs and anguish of his poor, weak mother, nor the unreasoning cries of a wife, tearing her hair and beating her white breast; but he would have liked to see a strong man who might refresh him with a word of wisdom, and cheer his end. And his strength failed him, and he cried in the weakness of his soul, " Father! where are you? do you hear? "

" I hear! " rang through the universal silence, and those thousands of people shuddered in concert. A detachment of cavalry hastened to search through the throng of people. Yankel turned pale as death, and when the horsemen had got within a short distance of him, turned round in terror to look for Taras; but Taras was no longer beside him; every trace of him was lost.

XII

THEY soon found traces of Taras. An army of a hundred and twenty thousand Cossacks appeared on the frontier of the Ukraine. This was no small detachment sallying forth for plunder or in pursuit of the Tatars. No: the whole nation had risen, for the measure of the people's patience was over-full; they had risen to avenge the disregard of their rights, the dishonourable humiliation of themselves, the insults to the faith of their fathers and their sacred customs, the outrages upon their church, the excesses of the foreign nobles, the disgraceful domination of the Jews on Christian soil, and all that had aroused and deepened the stern hatred of the Cossacks for a long time past. Hetman Ostranitza, young, but firm in mind, led the vast Cossack force. Beside him was seen his old and experienced friend and counsellor, Gunya. Ten leaders led bands of twelve thousand men each. Two osauls and a bunchúzhniy assisted the hetman. A cornet-general carried the chief standard, whilst many other banners and standards floated in the air; and the comrades of the staff bore the golden staff of the hetman, the symbol of his office. There were also many other officials belonging to the different bands, the baggage train and the main force with detachments of infantry and cavalry. There were almost as many free Cossacks and volunteers as there were registered Cossacks. The Cossacks had risen everywhere. They came from Tchigirin, from Pereyaslaf, from Baturin, from Glukhof, from the regions of the lower Dnieper, and from all its upper shores and islands. An uninterrupted stream of horses and herds of cattle stretched across the plain. And among all these Cossacks, among all these bands, one was the choicest; and that was the band led by Taras Bulba. All contributed to give him an influence over the others: his advanced years, his experience and skill in directing an army, and his bitter hatred of the foe. His unsparing fierceness and cruelty seemed exaggerated even to the Cossacks. His grey head dreamed of naught save fire and sword, and his utterances at the councils of war breathed only annihilation.

It is useless to describe all the battles in which the Cossacks distinguished themselves, or the gradual course of the campaign. All this is set down in the chronicles. It is well known what an army raised on Russian soil, for the orthodox faith, is like. There is no power stronger than faith. It is threatening and invincible like a rock, and rising amidst the stormy, ever-changing sea. From the very bottom of the sea it rears to heaven its jagged sides of firm, impenetrable stone. It is visible from everywhere, and looks the waves straight in the face as they roll past. And woe to the ship which is dashed against it! Its frame flies into splinters, everything in it is split and crushed, and the startled air re-echoes the piteous cries of the drowning.

In the pages of the chronicles there is a minute description of how the Polish garrisons fled from the freed cities; how the unscrupulous Jewish tavern-

keepers were hung; how powerless was the royal
hetman, Nikolai Pototzky, with his numerous army,
against this invincible force; how, routed and pursued,
he lost the best of his troops by drowning in a small
stream; how the fierce Cossack regiments besieged him
in the little town of Polon; and how, reduced to
extremities, he promised, under oath, on the part of
the king and the government, its full satisfaction to all,
and the restoration of all their rights and privileges.
But the Cossacks were not men to give way for this.
They already knew well what a Polish oath was worth.
And Pototzky would never more have pranced on his
six-thousand-ducat horse from the Kabardei, attracting
the glances of distinguished ladies and the envy of the
nobility; he would never more have made a figure in
the Diet, by giving costly feasts to the senators—if the
Russian priests who were in the little town had not saved
him. When all the popes, in their brilliant gold vestments, went out to meet the Cossacks, bearing the holy
pictures and the cross, with the bishop himself at their
head, crosier in hand and mitre on his head, the
Cossacks all bowed their heads and took off their caps.
To no one lower than the king himself would they have
shown respect at such an hour; but their daring fell
before the Church of Christ, and they honoured their
priesthood. The hetman and leaders agreed to release
Pototzky, after having extracted from him a solemn
oath to leave all the Christian churches unmolested,
to forswear the ancient enmity, and to do no harm to
the Cossack forces. One leader alone would not consent
to such a peace. It was Taras. He tore a handful of
hair from his head, and cried:

" Hetman and leaders! Commit no such womanish
deed. Trust not the Lyakhs; slay the dogs! "

When the secretary presented the agreement, and the
hetman put his hand to it, Taras drew a genuine
Damascene blade, a costly Turkish sabre of the finest
steel, broke it in twain like a reed, and threw the two
pieces far away on each side, saying, " Farewell! As

the two pieces of this sword will never reunite and form one sword again, so we, comrades, shall nevermore behold each other in this world. Remember my parting words." As he spoke his voice grew stronger, rose higher, and acquired a hitherto unknown power; and his prophetic utterances troubled them all. "Before the death hour you will remember me! Do you think that you have purchased peace and quiet? do you think that you will make a great show? You will make a great show, but after another fashion. They will flay the skin from your head, hetman, they will stuff it with bran, and long will it be exhibited at fairs. Neither will you retain your heads, gentles. You will be thrown into damp dungeons, walled about with stone, if they do not boil you alive in cauldrons like sheep. And you, men," he continued, turning to his followers, "which of you wants to die his true death? not through sorrows and womanish lounging, nor drunk under a hedge beside the ale-house; but an honourable Cossack death, all in one bed, like bride and groom? But, perhaps, you would like to return home, and turn infidels, and carry Polish priests on your backs?"

"We will follow you, noble leader, we will follow you!" shouted all his band, and many others joined them.

"If it is to be so, then follow me," said Taras, pulling his cap farther over his brows. Looking menacingly at the others, he went to his horse, and cried to his men, "Let no one reproach us with any insulting speeches. Now, hey there, men! we'll call on the Catholics." And then he struck his horse, and there followed him a camp of a hundred waggons, and with them many Cossack cavalry and infantry; and, turning, he threatened with a glance all who remained behind, and wrath was in his eye. The band departed in full view of all the army, and Taras continued long to turn and glower.

The hetman and leaders were uneasy; all became thoughtful, and remained silent, as though oppressed by some heavy foreboding. Not in vain had Taras prophesied: all came to pass as he had foretold. A little later, after the treacherous attack at Kaneva, the hetman's head was mounted on a stake, together with those of many of his officers.

And what of Taras? Taras made raids all over Poland with his band, burned eighteen towns and nearly forty churches, and reached Cracow. He killed many nobles, and plundered some of the richest and finest castles. The Cossacks emptied on the ground the century-old mead and wine, carefully hoarded up in lordly cellars; they cut and burned the rich garments and equipments which they found in the wardrobes. "Spare nothing," was the order of Taras. The Cossacks spared not the blackbrowed gentlewomen, the brilliant, white-bosomed maidens: these could not save themselves even at the altar, for Taras burned them with the altar itself. Snowy hands were raised to heaven from amid fiery flames, with piteous shrieks, which would have moved the damp earth itself to pity and caused the steppe-grass to bend with compassion at their fate. But the cruel Cossacks paid no heed; and, raising the children in the streets upon the points of their lances, they cast them also into the flames.

"This is a mass for the soul of Ostap, you heathen Lyakhs," was all that Taras said. And such masses for Ostap he had sung in every village, until the Polish Government perceived that Taras's raids were more than ordinary expeditions for plunder; and Pototzky was given five regiments, and ordered to capture him without fail.

Six days did the Cossacks retreat along the by-roads before their pursuers; their horses were almost equal to this unchecked flight, and nearly saved them. But this time Pototzky was also equal to the task intrusted to him; unweariedly he followed them, and overtook them on the bank of the Dniester, where Taras had taken possession of an abandoned and ruined castle for the purpose of resting.

On the very brink of the Dniester it stood, with its
shattered ramparts and the ruined remains of its walls.
The summit of the cliff was strewn with ragged stones
and broken bricks, ready at any moment to detach
themselves. The royal hetman, Pototzky, surrounded
it on the two sides which faced on the plain. Four days
did the Cossacks fight, tearing down bricks and stones
for missiles. But their stones and their strength were at
length exhausted, and Taras resolved to cut his way
through the beleaguering forces. And the Cossacks
would have cut their way through, and their swift
steeds might again have served them faithfully, had not
Taras halted suddenly in the very midst of their flight,
and shouted, " Halt! my pipe has dropped with its
tobacco: I won't let those heathen Lyakhs have my
pipe! " And the old hetman stooped down, and felt in
the grass for his pipe full of tobacco, his inseparable
companion on all his expeditions by sea and land and
at home.

But in the meantime a band of Lyakhs suddenly
rushed up, and seized him by the shoulders. He
struggled with all might; but he could not scatter on
the earth, as he had been wont to do, the heydukes
who had seized him. " Oh, old age, old age! " he
exclaimed: and the stout old Cossack wept. But his
age was not to blame: nearly thirty men were clinging
to his arms and legs.

" The raven is caught! " yelled the Lyakhs. " We
must think how we can show him the most honour, the
dog! " They decided, with the permission of the
hetman, to burn him alive in the sight of all. There
stood hard by a leafless tree, the summit of which had
been struck by lightning. They fastened him with iron
chains and nails driven through his hands high up on
the trunk of the tree, so that he might be seen from all
sides; and began at once to place fagots at its foot. But
Taras did not look at the wood, nor did he think of the
fire with which they were preparing to roast him: he
gazed anxiously in the direction whence his Cossacks

were firing. From his high point of observation he could see everything as in the palm of his hand.

"Take possession, men," he shouted, "of the hillock behind the wood: they cannot climb it!" But the wind did not carry his words to them. "They are lost, lost!" he said in despair, and glanced down to where the water of the Dniester glittered. Joy gleamed in his eyes. He saw the sterns of four boats peeping out from behind some bushes; exerted all the power of his lungs, and shouted in a ringing tone, "To the bank, to the bank, men! descend the path to the left, under the cliff. There are boats on the bank; take all, that they may not catch you."

This time the breeze blew from the other side, and his words were audible to the Cossacks. But for this counsel he received a blow on the head with the back of an axe, which made everything dance before his eyes.

The Cossacks descended the cliff path at full speed, but their pursuers were at their heels. They looked: the path wound and twisted, and made many *détours* to one side. "Comrades, we are trapped!" said they. All halted for an instant, raised their whips, whistled, and their Tatar horses rose from the ground, clove the air like serpents, flew over the precipice, and plunged straight into the Dniester. Two only did not alight in the river, but thundered down from the height upon the stones, and perished there with their horses without uttering a cry. But the Cossacks had already swum shoreward from their horses, and unfastened the boats, when the Lyakhs halted on the brink of the precipice, astounded at this wonderful feat, and thinking, "Shall we jump down to them, or not?"

One young colonel, a lively, hot-blooded soldier, own brother to the beautiful Pole who had seduced poor Andríi, did not reflect long, but leaped with his horse after the Cossacks. He made three turns in the air with his steed, and fell heavily on the rocks. The sharp stones tore him in pieces; and his brains, mingled with blood, bespattered the shrubs growing on the uneven walls of the precipice.

When Taras Bulba recovered from the blow, and glanced towards the Dniester, the Cossacks were already in the skiffs and rowing away. Balls were showered upon them from above but did not reach them. And the old hetman's eyes sparkled with joy.

"Farewell, comrades!" he shouted to them from above; "remember me, and come hither again next spring and make merry in the same fashion! What! cursed Lyakhs, have ye caught me? Think ye there is anything in the world that a Cossack fears? Wait; the time will come when ye shall learn what the orthodox Russian faith is! Already the people scent it far and near. A czar shall arise from Russian soil, and there shall not be a power in the world which shall not submit to him!" But fire had already risen from the fagots; it lapped his feet, and the flame spread to the tree. . . . But can any fire, flames, or power be found on earth which are capable of overpowering Russian strength?

Broad is the river Dniester, and in it are many deep pools, dense reed-beds, clear shallows and little bays; its watery mirror gleams, filled with the melodious plaint of the swan, the proud wild goose glides swiftly over it; and snipe, red-throated ruffs, and other birds are to be found among the reeds and along the banks. The Cossacks rowed swiftly on in the narrow double-ruddered boats—rowed stoutly, carefully shunning the sand bars, and cleaving the ranks of the birds, which took wing—rowed, and talked of their hetman.

END OF TARAS BULBA